Lincolnshire
COUNTY COUNCIL
Working for a better future

THE OSTRICH OF Pudding LANE

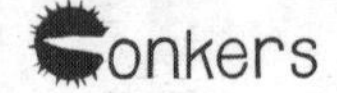

First published in 2016 in Great Britain by
Barrington Stoke Ltd
18 Walker Street, Edinburgh, EH3 7LP

www.barringtonstoke.co.uk

A CIP catalogue record for this book is available
from the British Library upon request

ISBN: 978-1-78112-552-6

Printed and bound by CPI Group (UK) Ltd, Croydon, CR0 4YY

THE OSTRICH of Pudding Lane

JEREMY STRONG

WITH ILLUSTRATIONS BY SARAH HORNE

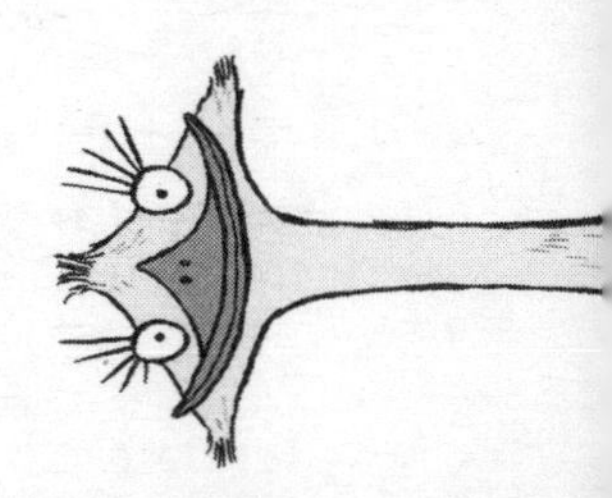

Conkers

I would like to thank all the Mad Irises,
animal and human, that brighten our lives.
We must treasure them.

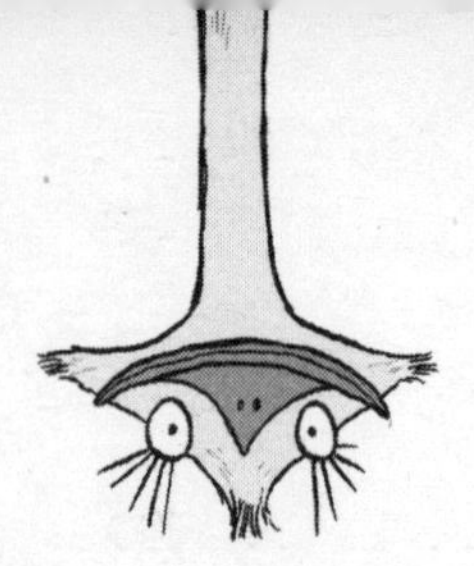

Contents

Chapter 1
Who Is K.J.?

The note in Ross's bag was short and simple.

> Do you want to go out with me?
>
> If you do, meet me after lunch
>
> by the conker tree.
>
> K.J.

Ross turned a deep red and quickly folded the note. He pushed it to the bottom of his bag. He didn't dare look up, so he stared at his book. His mind was racing. K.J.? That was the new girl – Kelly Jessup.

Kelly Jessup! Did Ross want to go out with *her*? Yes! Yes! Kelly made his legs turn to jelly. Kelly made his heart thump like a pounding drum. Kelly made ...

"Ross? Ross? Are you listening?" his teacher Mrs Norton said with a sigh. "I said, what do you call a triangle with three equal sides?"

"Kelly," Ross replied dreamily.

"Don't be so stupid. You can't call a triangle *Kelly*," Mrs Norton snapped.

The rest of the class were laughing, all except for Katie. She waved her arm in the air.

"I think it's a great idea," she said brightly. "We could give every shape a name. Squares could be called Norman, and circles could be called Tracy, and rectangles ..."

"Do stop being silly," Mrs Norton grumbled, while the rest of the class gazed at Katie as if she were truly weird.

"Roger," Katie went on. "Roger Rectangle. That would be a good name."

"Oh, give me strength!" Mrs Norton groaned. "A triangle with three equal sides is called ..."

But then her voice was drowned out by the bell for lunch.

Books were slammed back into desks or pushed into bags. Everyone made for the door.

Ross could hardly wait. Kelly Jessup – she was going to wait for him by the conker tree!

Ross bolted down his food and then sat on his chair in the hall, fretting. The dinner ladies wouldn't let him go until everyone had finished. Ross reckoned he would die of old age before that snail Gloria chomped her way through her rice pudding. At last she sucked down her last spoonful.

Ross dashed out to the playground but stopped before he got too close. 'Play it cool,' he told himself. 'Take it easy. Just walk across slowly.'

The conker tree came into view. Yes,

Kelly really was there! She was laughing at something Ian Tufnell was telling her.

Ross snorted. Ian was an idiot. OK, so maybe he was tall and good-looking and brilliant at judo. Apart from that, he was a total no-brain. Everyone knew that.

Ross drifted across and smiled at Kelly. She gave him a little frown. Ross raised his eyebrows at her several times.

"Is there something wrong with your eyebrows?" she asked.

"Yes! No! I mean the answer is yes!" Ross said with a grin.

"There *is* something wrong with your eyebrows?"

"No, not my eyebrows. The note. Yes is the answer to the note." Ross flashed his number one best smile.

All at once Ian was looming over Ross, who suddenly noticed what big hands Ian had.

"Why don't you go somewhere else?" Ian the judo expert growled.

But Ross didn't care about Ian. He was there for Kelly. He tried to look at her over Ian's broad shoulder.

"I do want to go out with you!" he shouted.

Ian's face turned to thunder. "You want to go out with *me*?"

Ross's heart sank. Why was Ian so stupid? "Not you – her! Kelly."

And that was when Ross's wonderful world turned into a hopeless pile of rubbish.

Kelly's eyes grew wide with horror. "Go out with you? You must be joking. I wouldn't go out with you if we were the last two people left on this planet."

Ian pushed Ross backwards. "Get lost, little boy. She's going out with me."

Ross's heart was shredded. It had been such a wonderful dream. He turned away, while Kelly and Ian sniggered at him.

A hand gently touched his arm and he looked up.

It was Katie.

She gave him a little smile.

"It's not that bad," she told him.

"It is," Ross muttered.

"The note wasn't from Kelly," she went on. "I didn't realise we had the same initials. K.J. It was from me."

"You!"

Katie smiled again, hopefully. "I put it in

your bag after Assembly this morning. What do you think?"

Ross was furious. He could not believe that he had got Kelly Jessup mixed up with Katie Jacobs. For heaven's sake – Katie Jacobs! The girl had freckles coming out of her ears! AND she was weird.

Ross turned on her. He was going to tell her that he wouldn't go out with her if they were the last two people left on the planet.

But he didn't. Instead his jaw dropped and he stared in stunned silence.

An ostrich had just come crashing through the school hedge.

An OSTRICH?????!!!!!

Now the giant bird was striding across

the playground. It was making straight for Katie and Ross, and it had a nasty glint in its eyes.

Chapter 2
Mad Iris

Ostriches are big birds, very big. When they are running straight at you they look even bigger. This one was like a huge black and white steam train, with feathers on all sides.

The children in the playground scattered in every direction. Mrs Norton, who was on playground duty, dived head-first into a bush.

She was not the only one. Kelly Jessup and Ian Tufnell were already in there.

While everyone else was screaming and

running away, Katie grabbed Ross and hissed at him, “Stand quite still!”

So Ross did as he was told. He couldn’t have run away even if he’d wanted to. (Which he did.) His legs had turned to jelly.

The ostrich stopped short, just one stride away from where the two children stood rooted to the spot. It fluttered its very long eyelashes and studied them carefully.

What strange birds ostriches are! They have feathers but they can't fly. Their knees are big and knobbly. They have the most odd-looking faces.

This ostrich stretched her neck forward and gently touched Ross's nose with her beak. He twitched.

"Hello," Katie said in a calm, quiet voice. "I like you."

"Don't be stupid!" Ross muttered. "You can't *like* an ostrich."

"Sssh," Katie went on, in the same soft voice. "Just speak to her nicely. Don't move suddenly. Do everything slowly."

Katie reached into her bag as she spoke. She pulled out a chocolate bar. She was going to unwrap it, but the ostrich snatched it from her hand and ate it just as it was.

Then the bird stuck her whole head into Katie's bag. It ate her ruler, her felt-tip pens and a spare pair of socks she had brought for P.E.

"Oh!" Katie said.

"Ha, ha," laughed Ross, too loudly. The ostrich lifted her head, looked at Ross for a

second and bit his ear. "Ow!" he yelled.

"Serves you right," said Katie, gently stroking the bird's bony head. "You're a clever ostrich, aren't you? Oh yes, and you are so beautiful. I shall call you Iris."

Ross almost choked. "You *can't* call her Iris! You're mad. *She's* mad!"

"Then I shall call her Mad Iris," Katie said with a smile, and she thought how it seemed a very good name for an ostrich.

Mrs Norton climbed out of the bush and grabbed a big broom. She began to creep up on the ostrich from behind.

"Come away from that bird," she told Katie and Ross.

"She's not dangerous," Katie pointed out, stroking Mad Iris's long neck. The ostrich closed her eyes. She loved it.

But Mrs Norton knew a lot better. Ostriches *were* dangerous. She had to get rid of it. She didn't want an ostrich in the school playground. She waved her broom.

"Shoo!" she shouted. "Shoo! Shoo! Shoo!"

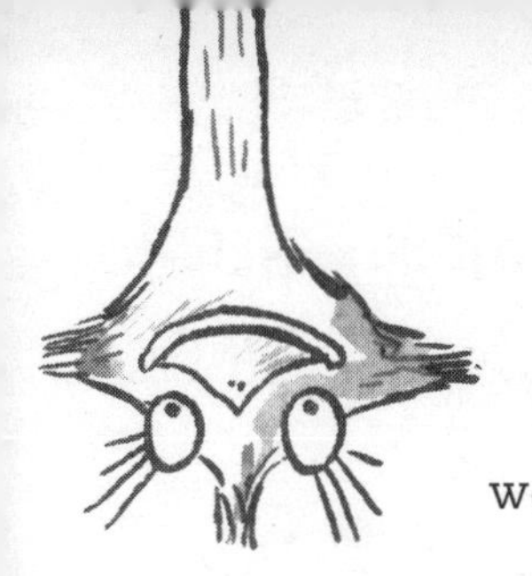

Mad Iris jerked her head up.

"You're scaring her," Katie warned.

"Shoo!" Mrs Norton yelled again, and she waved her broom again too.

Mad Iris took a step towards the teacher. Her head suddenly shot forward and she pulled the broom from Mrs Norton's hands. She tossed it on the ground, and with one mighty kick, she broke it in half and tossed it to the side.

Mrs Norton couldn't speak.

Mad Iris took another step towards her. What *was* that large, pink thing in the middle of her face? Mad Iris reached forward, grabbed Mrs Norton's nose in her beak and tried to yank it off.

"Ow! My dose! Let go of my dose!" Mrs Norton yelled, unable to breathe. She waved her arms and jumped up and down.

At last, Mad Iris let go, and the teacher sank to the ground. The ostrich stepped over the poor woman and strutted into the school.

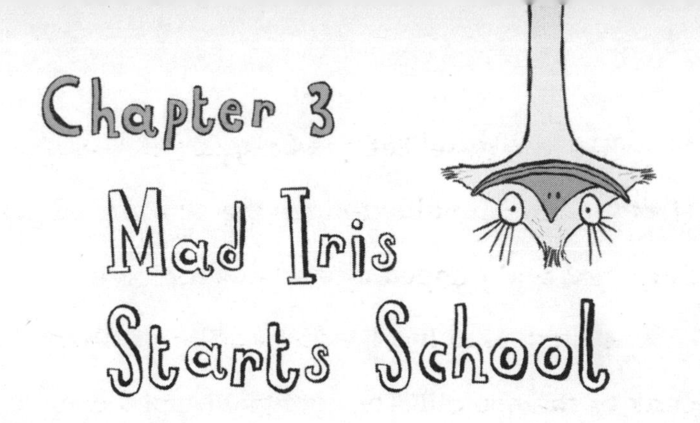

Chapter 3
Mad Iris Starts School

“Come on,” Katie said. “We’d better follow her.”

She grabbed Ross by the arm and pulled him after her, much to his amazement.

By this time, Mad Iris was marching up and down the corridors, poking her long beak in everywhere. She pushed her way into the caretaker’s little room and snatched his sandwiches right out of his hands.

In the school office, she had a go on Mrs Perch’s computer. Then she spread the neat piles of papers right around the office, so that she could see them more clearly.

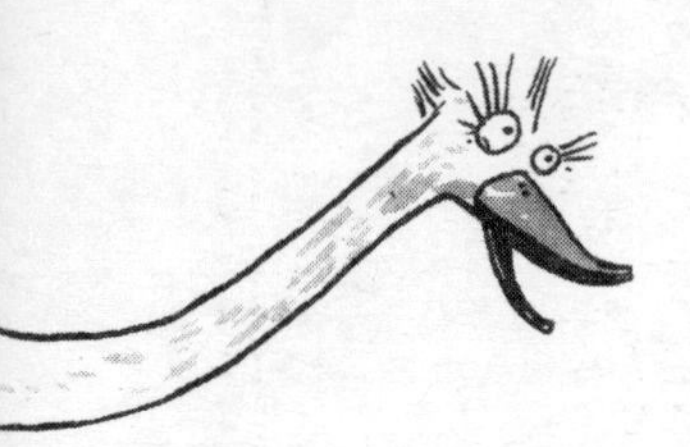

While this was going on, Mrs Perch tried to hide in her big cupboard.

In the end, the ostrich went and stood in the head teacher's office. Mr Grimble didn't even look up from his desk. He just muttered, "What do you want, boy?"

Mad Iris picked up Mr Grimble's phone and tried to swallow it.

That was when Mr Grimble raised his head and found himself gazing at an ostrich. The ostrich gazed back at him and fluttered her long eyelashes. Mad Iris spat out the phone, in several bits.

"Oh," Mr Grimble said carefully. Then he moved slowly across to the window. He opened it softly, while Mad Iris watched him with a beady eye.

Then the head teacher jumped out the window and ran off.

Mad Iris emptied Mr Grimble's filing cabinet and then went off to find Katie. The ostrich liked Katie. She had chocolate in her bag.

When she saw Mr Grimble jump out of the window, Katie decided Mad Iris was going to be great fun.

The ostrich followed Katie into her classroom. All the other children ducked behind the tables.

"We're going to keep her," Katie told them all, and she turned to Ross. "Aren't we?"

"Yes. We are." Ross couldn't believe what he was saying. Why was he agreeing with Katie

Jacobs? She was mad! He didn't even like her.

"You can't keep an ostrich in school," Kelly Jessup sneered from behind Ian Tufnell.

"You've got twigs in your hair," Katie said coolly. Ross felt himself smile.

Then Ian Tufnell surprised Ross by saying that he thought keeping an ostrich in school would be a terrific idea.

And Kelly Jessup surprised Ian by hitting him. "It's a stupid idea," Kelly snarled. "Katie's just weird. Anyhow, the teachers will never let you keep her. I bet they are on the phone to the police right now."

And she was right. By this time, the teachers, including Mr Grimble, had locked themselves in the staff room.

"It's as tall as Big Ben!" Mr Grimble shouted down the phone.

"It's got eight legs!" cried the caretaker.

"And six beaks!" squeaked Mrs Norton, who still had a very sore nose.

Mr Grimble put down the phone and turned to his staff. "It's all right," he said. "The police know all about that bird. It escaped from an ostrich farm. The keepers are on their way to the school right now. We shall soon get rid of it. Well then, who's for coffee? Any biscuits left?"

Outside the staff room door, Ross's friend Buster listened at the keyhole. They were going to get rid of their ostrich! He hurried back and passed on the news.

"We've got to save her," he told the class. "What shall we do?"

"We should hide her," said Gloria. "We must find somewhere that nobody will ever think of. It will have to be somewhere big enough to put an ostrich."

There was a deep silence. It was only broken by Mad Iris, who chose this moment to make a long and rather rude noise, before making a mess on the floor.

"Urrgh! That's revolting!" cried Ian.

"She doesn't know any better," Katie said.

Mad Iris seemed to agree with her because she now tried to eat Katie's hair.

"GET OFF!" Katie slapped the bird's head and Mad Iris began to eat Mrs Norton's felt-tip pens instead. Then she went back to Katie's hair, only her beak was full of felt-tip pens now. She left squiggly, brightly coloured marks all over Katie's head. "Stop it, you idiot!"

"I know what!" Ross cried. "We could put her in the toilet, and then it won't matter if she does a poo."

"You can't put an ostrich in a toilet," Kelly said with a sneer. "She won't fit."

Ross turned very red. "I don't mean *in* the toilet *itself* – in one of the booths. I bet nobody will think to look there. You'd never expect to find an ostrich in the boys' toilets, would you?"

"He's right, you know," Katie said with a grin. "Well done, Ross – you're not just a pretty face!"

Ross gave her a big grin.

"Ooooooooooh!" went the class, while Ross turned even redder.

Chapter 4
Anyone Want an Ostrich for Dinner?

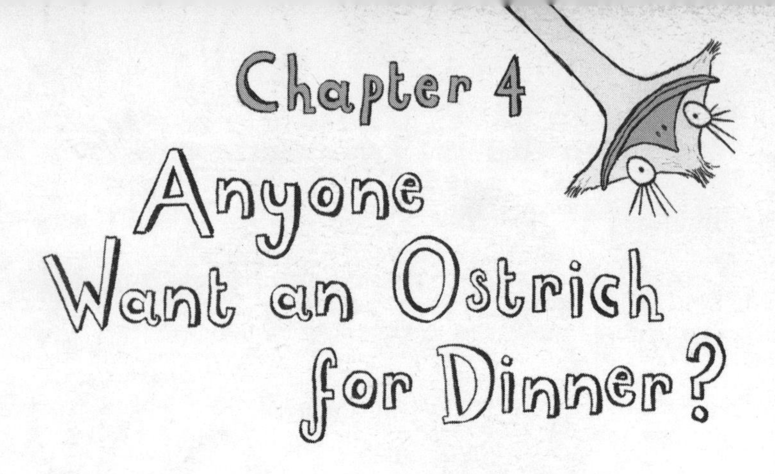

Mad Iris thought the toilets were very interesting.

First of all, she pulled the toilet roll off the holder and unrolled it. Then she wrapped the paper round the water tank, round the pipes, round the toilet bowl, round Ross's head, and round Buster's legs.

Finally, she tossed the roll over the top of the open door. Everyone thought this was very funny, even Ross.

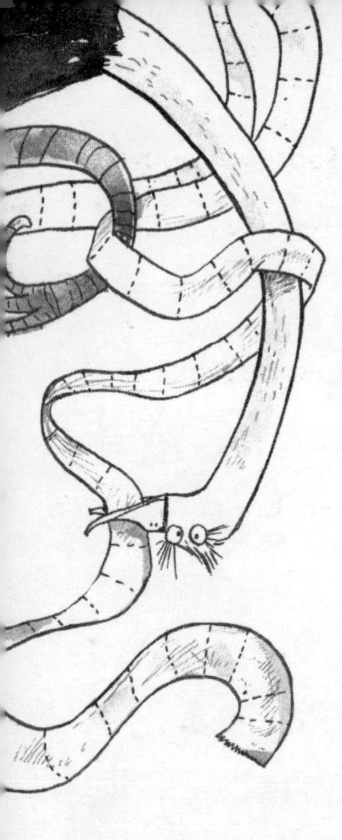

Mad Iris's next trick was to pull the toilet chain. Not only did the toilet flush, but the chain came off.

Mad Iris swallowed it.

By this time, nearly all the children in the toilets were falling about laughing. The best bit was when the ostrich got some loo paper stuck to her beak. When she groomed her feathers with her beak, it looked as if she was wiping herself.

Katie tried to be serious. She fixed Mad Iris with a stern gaze. "You've got to stay here and be very, very quiet. Do you understand?"

Mad Iris lifted one huge foot and plonked

it in a toilet pan. Katie lifted the foot back out and wagged her finger. "Will you behave?" she said. "You must keep quiet."

Katie had hardly finished when Buster came tearing down the corridor.

"There are some men coming!" he yelled. "Loads of them!"

From the far distance the children could hear the wail of sirens. It was getting louder. Then several police cars swept into the playground, followed by a fire engine. Did they really think that the ostrich was going to set fire to the school?

Then a big dark truck appeared. It slowed to a halt and several men in black leaped out. There was writing on the side of the truck.

"They've got guns!" Ross whispered. "They're going to kill our ostrich and turn her into steaks for dinner!"

They watched, white-faced, as Mr Grimble spoke to the men. They could hear every word through the open windows.

"She escaped from our farm yesterday," one of the men declared.

"What are you going to do?" asked the head teacher.

"These stun-guns fire a drug that will put her to sleep. After that, we'll take her back to the farm. She's going to be killed in the end anyhow. They all are. We send the ostrich meat to supermarkets all over the place. Tastes lovely!"

One of the men grinned at Mr Grimble and smacked his lips.

Mr Grimble took a step back. He certainly did not want an ostrich in his school, but he was not at all happy about what was going to happen.

"We shall have to move the children out first," he told the men. "The staff can take the register in the playground to make sure everyone is out of the building before you go in. And don't tell the children what you plan to do. It will only upset them."

But it was too late.

The children knew, and they were already upset.

"Now what do we do?" Gloria wailed. "If

we're taken outside, there will be nobody to look after Mad Iris."

They stared at each other, their faces glum. From the far end of the school came the sound of their teachers, calling for them.

One by one they went back to their classes and still nobody had thought of a plan.

The teachers lined the children up along the corridors and led them outside. Soon the school was oddly silent and empty.

At least ... it was *almost* empty.

There was still an ostrich in a toilet cubicle, plonking one foot in and out of a toilet pan.

And hiding in a cloakroom, with their feet showing beneath some coats, were Ross and Katie.

The men in black picked up their stun-guns and strode into the school.

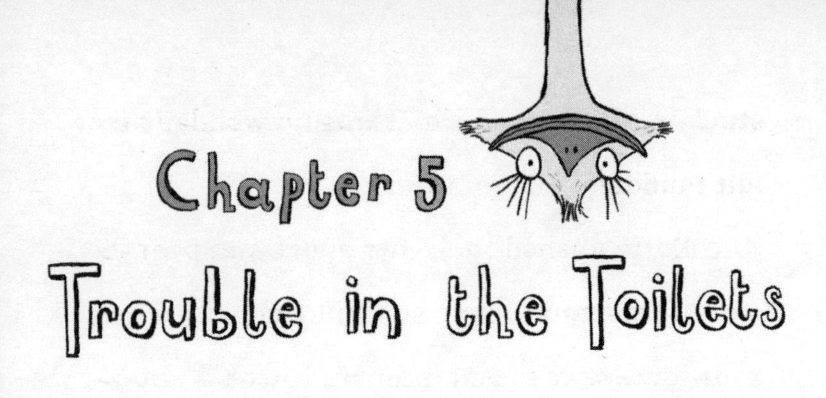

Chapter 5
Trouble in the Toilets

Ross and Katie huddled together in silence. Ross could hear Katie breathing fast. He reached down, found her hand and squeezed it. She squeezed back and didn't let go.

Ross shifted his feet and felt nervous. He didn't want to give Katie the wrong idea. On the other hand, he had no idea what the wrong idea was – or the right one, for that matter.

Here he was, standing under some coats, with a girl holding his hand and an ostrich stuck in a toilet cubicle. It was no wonder he felt muddled.

Katie pushed the coats apart and peered out. All seemed to be clear, but they could hear loud voices some way off. It would not be long before the men in black headed their way.

There was a terrible banging from the toilet. Ross dashed across to see what was going on. Mad Iris had discovered how to put the toilet lid down. And up. And down. And up again.

Bang bang bang bang!

"Stop it!" Ross hissed. "The men in black will hear you!"

Mad Iris stopped banging. Instead, she tried to eat the buttons on Katie's shirt. They wouldn't come off, so she had a go at Ross's ears instead. Ross threw up his arms to protect himself. "Ouch!" he said.

Katie giggled.

"It hurt!" Ross growled angrily.

"There, there. Shall I kiss it better for you?"

"No! I've just had an ostrich pecking my ear. I'm not going to let you have a go at it too!"

The smile suddenly vanished from Katie's face.

"Sssh, listen!" she said. "I think someone is coming this way."

Ross quietly closed the toilet door and went out into the corridor.

He instantly flung himself back inside. Someone *was* coming! A large, heavy man was marching down the corridor checking every room, one by one!

Ross dashed back to make sure the ostrich was well hidden. Her feet could just about be seen through the gap between the door and floor, but there was nothing he could do about that.

"Stay very, very still. Don't say a word," Ross whispered to Katie. "We're going to hide in the next-door toilet, OK?"

Mad Iris watched these strange children carefully. Why did they keep whispering? Something was going on. She decided to wait and see what happened next.

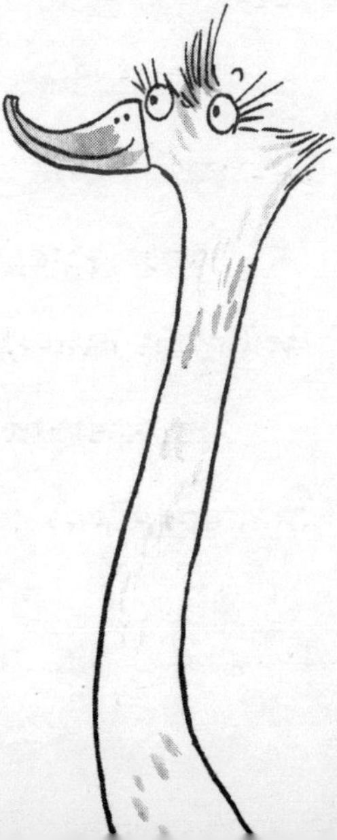

Ross and Katie slipped into the next-door toilet cubicle. Ross put down the toilet lid as softly as he could and then he climbed onto it.

"They mustn't be able to see our feet," he whispered, and Katie climbed up after him. Katie chose that moment to get a fit of the giggles and she started spluttering into her hand.

"Now what?" Ross demanded.

"I was just wondering what Mr Grimble would say if he opened this door and found us standing here."

Ross rolled his eyes. How come he was stuck in the boys' toilets with this crazy girl? He pulled himself up so that he could see over the wall into the ostrich's cubicle. At least *she* was behaving herself for once. Good.

The man out in the corridor was a big burger of a man. He had a big, round chest. He had a big, round face sitting on a big, round neck, all of which came from eating lots of burgers. He had just eaten one for lunch. He burped loudly as he wandered down the corridor, checking the rooms, with his stun-gun at the ready.

Big Burger Man was talking to himself. "Is there anyone in here?" he asked.

The children heard a door bang as it was flung open.

"No one in *that* room!" Big Burger Man said.

"Oho ho, I can see you! Peek a boo! Is

there anyone in here?" he went on. "No one in there either."

Bang went another door.

The door to the boys' toilets crashed open.

"Oh me, oh my, it's a tiddly room for tiddlers!" Big Burger Man sniggered. "I guess I'd better check the cubicles."

Ross held his breath and Katie shut her

eyes. The door of the toilet at the far end was opened.

"Nope," Big Burger Man muttered.

The next door opened.

"Nope," Big Burger Man said.

Then he opened the third door and found himself eye-to-beak with an ostrich.

"Ha! Got you!" Big Burger Man cried, and he made a grab for his gun.

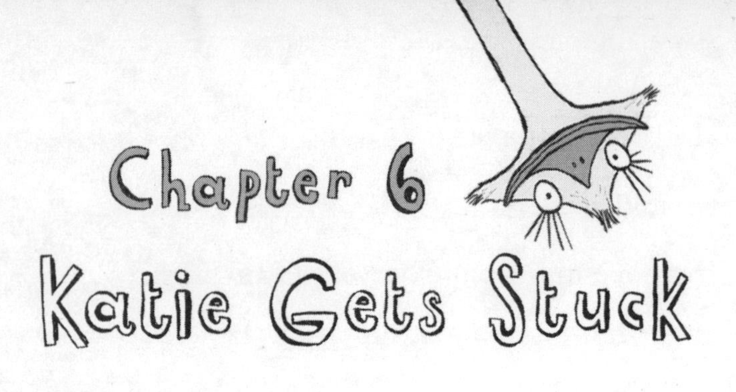

Chapter 6
Katie Gets Stuck

That was when Mad Iris decided to change Big Burger Man's face a bit. She tried to pull off his nose and ears. That didn't work, so she tried to pull out his hair, and with that she was a lot more successful.

"Ow! Yow! You pesky chicken!"

Big Burger Man staggered back, while Mad Iris banged the toilet lid several times to show how cross she was.

Big Burger Man took aim with his stun-gun.

"Yeee-hah!"

Ross flung himself over the top of the door and landed on Big Burger Man's shoulders. He clamped his hands over the man's eyes.

Katie jumped up and down on the toilet seat. “Get him, Ross! Go on! Pull his head off!”

KRAK!

The plastic lid snapped in half and Katie’s feet vanished into the bowl. A great spout of water jetted up over the sides. Katie couldn’t move. Her feet were firmly wedged in the toilet pan.

Big Burger Man clawed at Ross with one hand, but Ross held on for dear life. Mad Iris joined in and began pecking at the man’s clothes. Several rips appeared.

Big Burger Man staggered around, with Ross still on his back. He stumbled out into the corridor.

"GET OFF!" he yelled. "You horrible baboon!"

At last he dropped his stun-gun on the floor, pulled Ross from his shoulders and hurled him to the floor.

"Now I'll get that bird!" Big Burger Man hissed. "Where's my gun?"

Mad Iris had it. The ostrich liked big, shiny things. She kicked the gun around with her feet. She pecked it with her beak. And that was when it went off.

Bing!

A little stun-dart shot out and stuck in

Big Burger Man's ankle.

"You ...!" was all he could manage to say before he slumped to the ground.

Ross struggled to his feet. "Come on, Katie, we can't stay here. The others must have heard us by now. We'll hide upstairs."

Katie's face was white. "I can't move," she said. "My feet are stuck. Take Mad Iris and go before the others get here. I'll be OK. Go on, go, go, GO!"

Ross stared at her for a second and then nodded. He pulled Mad Iris out into the corridor and dashed up the steps.

Mad Iris lolloped after him. Somehow the ostrich sensed that Ross was on her side. In fact, Ross was probably her only hope now.

Ross searched wildly for a hiding place. He heard footsteps and voices below. The only door they could go through now led onto the school's flat roof. Nobody, not even Mr Grimble, was allowed out onto that roof. It was far too dangerous.

"There they are!" cried one of the men.

Ross began to panic. What could he do now? Mad Iris gazed all around. What was that big, red, shiny thing on the wall? It looked tasty! Mad Iris pecked at it. Hard.

Clang-a-lang-a-lang-a-lang!!

Alarms clattered. Water showered madly down from the ceiling. Mad Iris had set off the fire alarm and water sprinklers.

The men in black backed off for a

moment, as water soaked through their clothes. Ross seized his chance. He opened the door onto the flat roof and pushed the ostrich through. Then he shut it behind him.

They stood on a big, flat, empty space. There was nowhere else to hide and nowhere else to go. They were all alone on top of the school, with the wind whistling in Ross's ears. He peered over the edge. The other children seemed miles away, like little matchstick people.

Ross stood on the roof with the ostrich, and he felt alone and helpless and afraid.

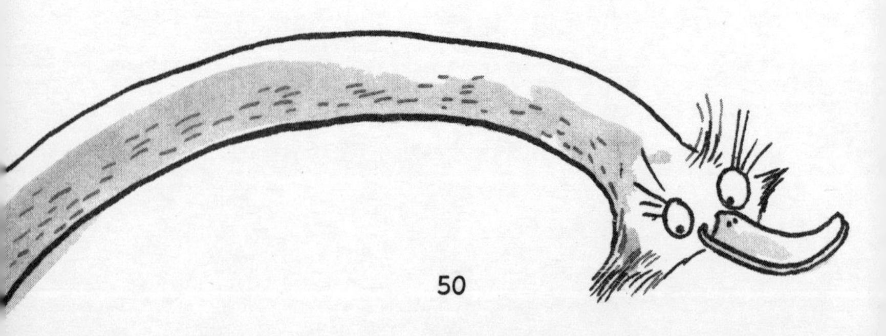

Then the door burst open and several dripping men squelched out onto the roof.

"Game's over, boy! Don't move!" one yelled.

Ross turned to the ostrich at his side. "Fly!" he yelled. "Fly for your life!"

Chapter 7 An Unexpected Surprise

But, of course, ostriches can't fly.

Mad Iris was scared and she did what ostriches do when they are scared. She hid her head. She plunged her head down Ross's shirt.

The men took several steps closer.

"Just keep very still, boy," one of the men ordered. "That's a very dangerous bird you've got next to you."

"She isn't dangerous!" Ross cried. "You've got guns! You're the ones who are dangerous."

“Don’t be stupid now. Just take one step this way, so we can get a good shot at the chicken.”

“She’s an ostrich,” Ross snapped. He twisted round so that he was standing between Mad Iris and the men.

"Are you always such a pain?" one of them snapped.

"You're a bigger pain than me," Ross replied.

"Wise guy, huh?"

The men were getting cross. Ross knew this stand-off couldn't last for ever. Something would have to happen soon, and it did. The head teacher poked his head over the roof.

While everyone had been talking, the fire engine had raised its ladder. Mr Grimble had climbed up and now he clambered over the edge of the roof.

Ross sighed. The game was up. He would have to give in now. There was nothing more he could do.

The men in black grinned.

"Thank you, sir," said their leader. "If you could just remove the boy from our line of fire we'll deal with the chicken right away."

Mr Grimble stepped closer to Ross. He put a hand on his shoulder and gripped it hard. Ross's heart sank.

Mr Grimble eyed the five men. "We are not going to move anywhere yet," he said. "You can put down your guns and leave this building at once. I am in charge here and I want you off these school grounds in five minutes."

"But ..." one of the men began.

"No buts," Mr Grimble insisted. "The chicken, as you call it, will stay here with us."

“That ostrich is ours,” cried the men.

“No, she isn’t,” Mr Grimble said with a smile. “I’ve just bought her for the school. We’re going to keep her as our lucky mascot and we’re going to look after her. Goodbye!”

The men backed off, muttering.

As they vanished from the roof, Ross realised that the whole school was cheering in the playground below. They were shouting and laughing and waving their arms, even Mrs Norton.

Mr Grimble, Ross and Mad Iris stood on the roof, together. Ross felt madly happy. Mad Iris just felt mad. She undid Mr Grimble’s shoelaces.

“Behave yourself,” the head teacher

snapped. "If you don't, I shall … oh! She's eaten my glasses." Then Mr Grimble sighed. "I think it should have stopped raining indoors by now," he said. "Shall we go inside?"

Ross smiled. He thought that was a very good idea. They were half way down the stairs when Ross suddenly remembered Katie. He wondered what Mr Grimble would say. Perhaps it would be better not to tell him? On the other hand, Ross couldn't just leave Katie in the boys' toilets.

"I think I'd better show you something," Ross said as they reached the toilets.

Shouting came from inside.

"Ross! Are you out there? If you leave me here for ever, I shall never hold hands with you again!"

Mr Grimble looked at Ross and his eyebrows slowly moved up his forehead.

Chapter 8 Ross Makes Up His Mind

"That sounds like a girl," Mr Grimble said, and Ross nodded glumly. "Why is there a girl in the boys' toilets?"

"I think you'd better take a look," Ross suggested, and so Mr Grimble went in.

"Ross!" Katie shouted. "If you get me out you can kiss me if you want!"

Mr Grimble's eyebrows rose even higher. Ross went scarlet and gave a little shrug.

"Girls," he said. "What can you do?"

The head teacher pushed open the door. Katie still had both feet firmly stuck in the toilet pan. She gave Mr Grimble a pale smile. "Oh! I thought it was Ross."

"So it seems."

Katie hardly dared ask, but she had to know. "Did you hear what I just said?"

"About Ross and ...?" Mr Grimble broke off and shook his head. "Didn't hear a word," he said. "We'd better get you out, hadn't we?"

It took half an hour of struggling to free Katie's feet from the toilet pan. Mad Iris tried to help by pulling the chain several times. She wrapped Mr Grimble in toilet paper. Finally,

when he lost his temper and shouted at her to stop, the ostrich plunged her head down the back of his jacket and hid.

At last, Katie was able to stand on dry ground. Her feet and ankles were a bit sore, but otherwise she was fine.

They all went out onto the playground, where they were greeted with huge cheers. Mad Iris strutted this way and that, looking very proud of herself, even though she hadn't done anything useful.

Kelly Jessup came over to Ross with a winning smile and laid a hand on his arm.

"You were just *so* brave," she said. "And clever. You can go out with me if you want."

Ross looked across to where Katie Jacobs was talking to Mad Iris. Katie Jacobs! She had freckles coming out of her ears. Her face was covered with felt-tip pen. She was friends with an ostrich. She was mad.

Ross smiled at Kelly. "I'm with her," he said. "And the ostrich."

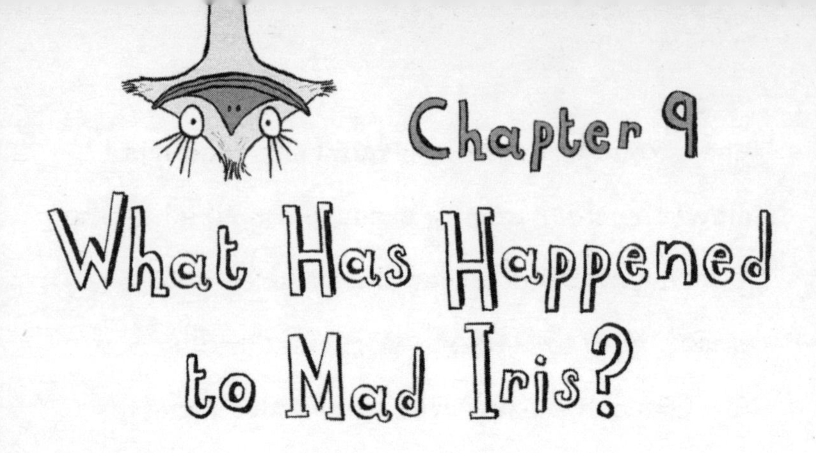

Chapter 9
What Has Happened to Mad Iris?

As you know, not every school has an ostrich. But that's what made Pudding Lane Primary a very special school – they *did* have an ostrich. They had Mad Iris. She wasn't a pretend ostrich and she wasn't a toy ostrich or a stuffed one either. She was a very real ostrich.

Mad Iris liked it a lot at Pudding Lane School.

The children at Pudding Lane liked Mad Iris, because she ate their pencils and then they couldn't do their schoolwork. Mad Iris liked the children too, because she liked eating pencils. And this is why the children made sure that Mad Iris stayed at their school.

Ross and Katie were Mad Iris's best friends at school, but Katie *said* that she was Ross's girlfriend too, but Ross said no, they were just ordinary friends. Who do you think was right?

Now that Mad Iris was the school mascot, she lived in the caretaker's shed. The caretaker didn't think this was the right place for an ostrich to live, but he couldn't get rid of her. He had to find somewhere else to go, so he shared the cook's little office with her. He liked that, and the cook liked that, and soon they got married – but that's another story.

Mad Iris liked the caretaker's old shed because it was full of interesting things that made interesting noises when she chewed them. They often had interesting tastes, too. For example, she might eat a bit of rubber tube. It made squeaky noises in her beak and it tasted of ... well, it tasted of rubber, of course.

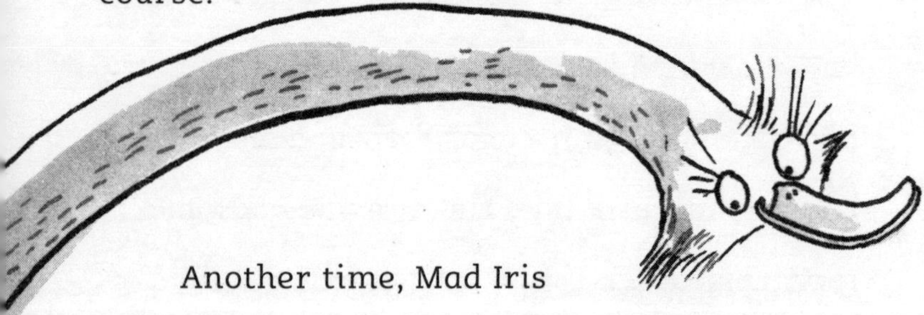

Another time, Mad Iris might eat a small pack of screws. Mad Iris didn't know if she liked eating screws. They were a bit hard to chew, but she liked the way they sparkled. She tried to eat the screwdriver too, because somehow it seemed to go with the screws. Mad Iris was certain she did *not* like the screwdriver. It was too pointy and sharp. She spat it out. Then she stamped on it and kicked it under a cupboard so she wouldn't have to think about it any more.

Everyone at Pudding Lane liked having an ostrich as their school mascot. No other school had anything like Mad Iris. Bottom End Primary had a fluffy pink teddy for their mascot. Top End Primary *said* they had a real shark for their mascot. They *said* they kept it in the school swimming pool. Nobody at Pudding Lane believed them of course, except the five-year-olds in Year 1. But then most of the children in Year 1 also believed that Mr Grimble had special superhero powers. He didn't.

So, the children at Pudding Lane Primary were very happy, and so was Mad Iris.

But then, one morning, Ross and Katie and their friends went to say "Hello" to Mad Iris, like they did every morning before school. They opened the shed door and she wasn't there.

MAD IRIS HAD VANISHED!

Chapter 10

Ross Does Some Thinking

"Where is Mad Iris?" Katie asked.

"I don't know," Ross snapped. How should he know? He spotted a scrap of paper on the floor and picked it up. "It's a note," he said.

"What does it say?" asked Ross's friend, Buster.

"It says 'HA HA'," a puzzled-looking Ross told Katie and Buster.

"Ha ha?" repeated Katie. "What's that supposed to mean?"

Ross looked at her and frowned. "I suppose it means 'HA HA', like in *HA HA*. How am I supposed to know what 'HA HA' means? That's all it says."

"Someone is playing a trick on us," Katie said in a growly voice, and Buster nodded.

"Do you think the teachers are having a joke?" he asked.

They went to see Mrs Norton, who was their class teacher. They told her that Mad Iris had vanished. Mrs Norton was very surprised and said she didn't know anything about it. Then they all went to see the head teacher, Mr Grimble.

Mr Grimble hurried to the empty shed and peered inside. "Oh dear," he muttered.

"She must have escaped."

"She left a note," Buster said.

"Don't be silly," Ross said. "Mad Iris can't write! Somebody else left the note, and that means somebody else was here." He showed Mr Grimble the scrap of paper.

"HA HA," read Mr Grimble. "Do you know what? I think Mad Iris has been kidnapped."

"Kidnapped?" echoed Ross and Katie. "Why would anyone want to kidnap an ostrich?"

"I don't know," said Mr Grimble, "but it's happened at the very worst time. We've got the football final against Top End Primary at the end of this week. They've won the cup every year so far. They always beat us in the final."

"That's because they cheat," Katie said. She was angry. Katie was one of the stars of the football team.

"Maybe they do," Mr Grimble agreed. "Even so, I was hoping we would beat them this year. I thought Mad Iris would bring us good luck. If she was watching we might win this year. It would be brilliant if we could beat Top End at last!"

Ross was looking down at the ground. He was thinking hard. He frowned a bit. Then he frowned a bit more and then he frowned a lot.

"What's up with you?" asked Buster.

"I've been thinking," Ross said. "It's odd that Mad Iris has been kidnapped just when we need her most." The frown vanished and he smiled. "Who would want to do that?" he asked.

"Who?" Mrs Norton demanded. "We don't know. Do you?"

“I think I have a pretty good idea,” Ross said.

“Stop messing about and tell us then!” shouted the others.

Ross smiled again. “Top End Primary, of course. It’s just the sort of nasty trick they would pull. They’ve stolen Mad Iris to make sure that we play badly on Friday.”

Mr Grimble looked at Mrs Norton. “He could be right,” he said with a nod.

Mrs Norton looked at Buster. “He could be right,” she agreed.

Buster looked at Katie. “He could be right,” he said.

Katie beamed a big smile at Ross. “You are so clever. I always knew you were brainy as well as good looking."

"Oooh!" Mrs Norton said, with a twinkle in her eye. "Who's a lucky boy?"

Ross stopped smiling. He scowled instead, and while he scowled his face turned very, very red. Because secretly he was very, very pleased!

Mr Grimble stamped back to his office. "I am going to speak to the head teacher of Top End Primary," he said. "I am going to ring her up right now and ask for our ostrich back."

Chapter 11
Trouble at Top End Primary

The head teacher of Top End Primary was called Miss Sly.

When Mr Grimble rang she was having a grand time. This was because Mad Iris was in her office. The ostrich liked telephones. She liked to stick them into interesting places, like cups of coffee.

But the thing that Mad Iris liked best was to pick the telephone up and bang it on hard things like table tops and Miss Sly's head.

Miss Sly's head made lovely noises when Mad Iris hit it with a telephone. It went "OW!" and "STOPPITT!"

All this made life very difficult for Miss Sly. It made it very hard to have a proper talk with Mr Grimble.

"Why on earth would we want to steal your ostrich, Mr Grimble?" she snapped as she tried to stop Mad Iris from grabbing the phone.

"Because you want to stop us from winning the football cup on Friday," Mr Grimble said.

"You're being ridiculous," Miss Sly hissed. "*Gerroff!*" She waved a frantic hand at Mad Iris, so the ostrich pecked it. "Ow!"

Then Mad Iris grabbed the phone in her beak and shook it hard to see if it rattled. It didn't. How boring. Mad Iris decided to hide

the phone. She stuffed it inside Miss Sly's shirt.

"Wargh! Argh!" Miss Sly screamed.

The school secretary hurried into Miss Sly's office. She screamed too. The school secretary wasn't being attacked or anything. She just *liked* screaming.

"Aargh!"

So now they were both screaming and Mad Iris thought it was wonderful. The ostrich got rather excited and decided to chase Miss Sly and her secretary up and down the corridor for a bit.

At the other end of the line Mr Grimble listened to the screams. He smiled and put down his phone. Only one thing could cause so much trouble – Mad Iris. Now he was quite sure that Top End Primary had kidnapped the ostrich of Pudding Lane.

But how on earth could Pudding Lane get their mascot back?

"We should go straight over there and get her," said Mrs Norton.

Mr Grimble shook his head. "We can't just march into someone else's school and ask for our ostrich back," he said. "They'll call the police and we might get arrested. Anyway, I expect they'll hide Mad Iris somewhere until the match is over and done with."

The two teachers looked at each other and they both gave a long sigh. They couldn't think what to do.

Chapter 12 Who Is Monstermash?

Mr Grimble and Mrs Norton couldn't think of a plan to rescue Mad Iris. So that left everything up to Ross and his class. They talked about it all through break time. Ian Tufnell came up with an idea.

"Let's burst into Top End Primary and grab her," he suggested, with a warlike glint in his eye.

"The teachers will stop us," Katie pointed out.

"No, they won't. We'll tie them to their chairs."

Katie sighed. "Ian," she said, "there are lots more of them than there are of us. They'll overpower us. If anyone gets tied to chairs, it will be us!"

"She's right," Buster said with a nod.

"No way," said Ian. "I can do judo. They'll never tie me down."

"Yeah? Well, I can do origami," Ross said, and he winked at Katie.

Katie started to laugh. "Origami is paper-folding!" she said. "How's that going to help?"

It'll give them a surprise," Ross

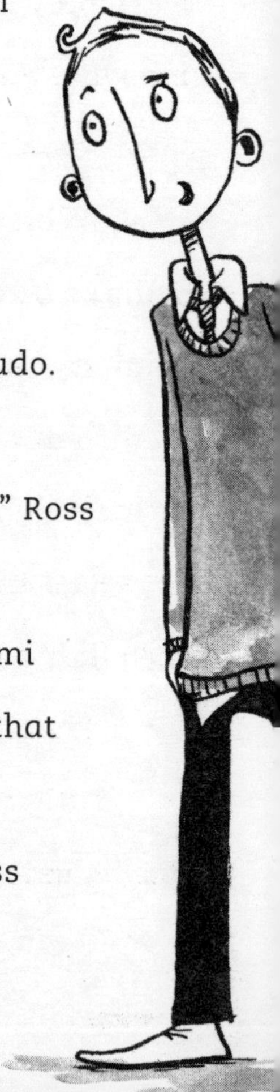

said with a chuckle. “And while the teachers are being surprised by my origami skills, you can rescue Mad Iris.”

Ian Tufnell stared at Katie and Ross moodily. He couldn’t see what was funny at all. “You’re stupid,” he muttered.

“Yeah, and so is trying to use your judo skills to beat up all the teachers at Top End Primary,” Ross pointed out.

“So what’s your plan then, clever clogs?” Ian asked.

Ross and Katie looked at each other. No, they didn’t have a plan.

“Idiots,” Ian growled, and he slunk off.

Katie waited until Ian was out of the way. Then she told Ross and Buster that, in fact, she *did* have a plan. "We'll have to break into the school and rescue Mad Iris. We could do it in the middle of the night."

Buster didn't think this idea would work. "The school will have loads of alarms. We'll never get in without setting them off."

"Suppose we did it really quickly? Maybe we could get in and out before the police arrive," said Ross.

But Buster shook his head again. It was too risky.

Katie suddenly grabbed their arms. Her eyes shone. "How about we just walk in? We go in like everyone else at the beginning of the day. If we wear the Top End school uniform nobody will notice us."

"Where are we going to get Top End uniforms from?" Ross asked.

Katie was almost jumping up and down with excitement. "That boy next door to you! He goes to Top End. His mum washes his uniform and hangs it on the line in the back garden to dry. All you have to do is nip over the fence and nick it!"

Ross suddenly understood Katie's plan. And he saw the whole horror of it. You see, Katie was right. His next-door neighbour did go to Top End, but Katie had left out something very important.

"That boy next door is called Monstermash," Ross groaned.

"Why?" Buster asked.

“Because he’s a monster and he mashes people,” Ross replied. “So now I have to steal a school uniform from a maniac, get into Top End school, find Mad Iris and rescue her. I am going to get totally murdered.” Ross sat down and sighed. “Great.”

Katie stroked his arm and smiled. “Don’t worry,” she said. “I’ll kiss it better for you.”

“Oh double great,” Ross said, with an even bigger sigh.

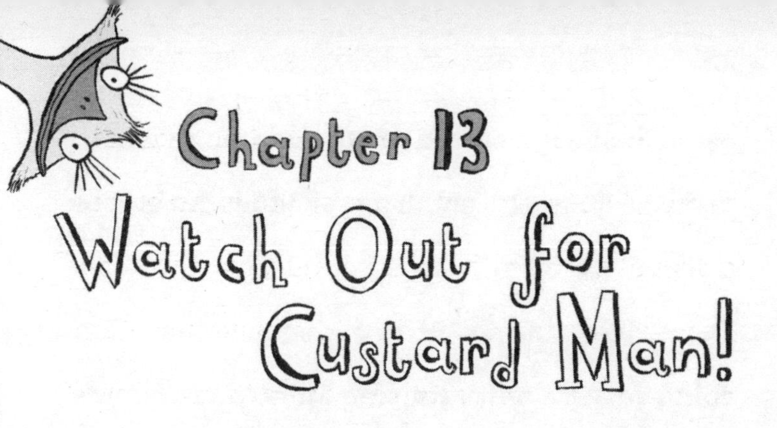

Chapter 13
Watch Out for Custard Man!

Meanwhile, in Top End Primary, Mad Iris had decided that this school was not nearly as much fun as Pudding Lane. She had also decided that if Top End wasn't going to make any fun for her, then she would have to make fun for them.

The first thing Mad Iris did was to take Assembly. As you probably know, ostriches are not supposed to take Assembly.

However, Mad Iris was a very special

ostrich. She waited until Miss Sly was standing in front of all the children. Then Mad Iris took control.

“Please stand,” Miss Sly said to the children. “We will now sing *Morning has* … waaaaargh!”

Mad Iris’s head had suddenly popped up behind Miss Sly. Mad Iris grabbed the song book from the head teacher and threw it at the front row.

“I’ll save you!” cried Mr Dubbin, the deputy head. He jumped up and ran over to Mad Iris. Somehow he landed on top of her back. Mad Iris took off at once, with Mr Dubbin clinging to her neck.

Off she went, racing away down the

corridor. SPLIP! SPLAP! went her enormous feet as she raced off.

"Help!" yelled Mr Dubbin. "I'm being kidnapped by an ostrich!"

Mad Iris dashed into the school kitchen and the cooks began screaming.

"Help! Alien invaders from Mars!" they shouted. They dropped all their pots and pans.

Mad Iris didn't like that horrible noise. She did what ostriches do when they are scared. She hid her head. She stuffed her head into a giant bowl of cold custard so that she couldn't hear anything.

It was bad luck that Mr Dubbin was still clinging to her back. He slid down her thin scrawny neck, hit the edge of the custard bowl

and then fell on the floor. The custard bowl wobbled for a moment, then tipped its contents over Mr Dubbin's head. Even Mad Iris was surprised. Where had the custard bowl gone? A minute ago she had felt safe, her head hidden inside it.

"You useless idiots!" cried the cooks. "You've ruined the pudding now! Get out!" They picked up their egg whisks and big wooden spoons and chased Mr Dubbin and Mad Iris back out into the corridor.

Mad Iris went splatting back to the hall, shaking the custard from her head. Behind her

was Mr Dubbin. And behind him were three very cross cooks.

All of them burst into the hall, where Miss Sly was trying to calm all the children down. Now they all began screaming again. A sloppy yellow monster was on the loose! And a mad ostrich! Teachers and children scattered

in all directions. Some climbed up the wall-bars in the hall. Some hid behind chairs.

Poor Mr Dubbin could hardly see where he was going because his eyes were full of custard. (So were his ears and nose and just about every other part of him.) He kept bumping into people.

Mad Iris was still trying to get away from all the noise. At last she found a small, quiet room with nobody in it. It was the library. Mad Iris peered at all the books. They looked very nice. Would they taste nice too? She ate one, and it did. So she ate another.

Suddenly there was a terrible noise from the far end of the corridor. A sloppy yellow maniac came charging towards her. Behind the madman were three cooks, now hurling plates and spoons and forks at him.

"STOP THIS NONSENSE AT ONCE!" roared Miss Sly. Then she was hit by a flying saucer. (A real flying saucer!) She crumpled into a heap on the floor.

So that was the end of Assembly at Top End Primary.

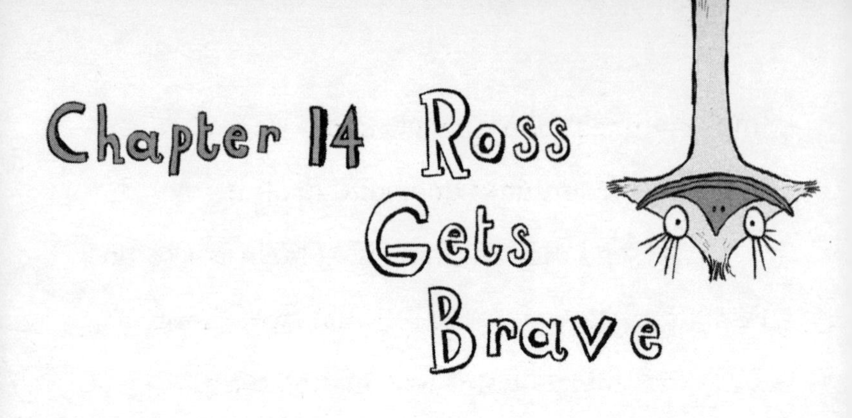

Chapter 14 Ross Gets Brave

In an odd way, Mad Iris had already done something that was going to help Ross a lot. Half the children from Top End Primary went home splattered with custard. Monstermash was one of them. His mum made him take off his uniform at once. It went straight into the washing machine. An hour later it was hanging out to dry on the line in the garden.

Ross waited until it was getting dark. He knew that Monstermash's mum would take the uniform back indoors very soon. He had to get into the garden next door and grab it.

"OK," he said to himself. "I have got to do this. I shall count to three. One, two, three ..."

Ross bit his lip. It was no good. He couldn't do it. He stayed in his own garden.

"I must be brave," he told himself. "I'll count to three, and then I'll do the final countdown, and then I'll do it. Right. Here we go. One, two, three ... and final countdown ... three, two, one, a half, a quarter, er ... ZERO! GO! GO! GO!"

Ross jumped up onto the fence and dropped down into next-door's garden. He raced across the grass. He grabbed the sweatshirt, pulled the trousers off the line and

dashed back. He was back over the fence again in one jump and he did three victory laps round his own garden.

“I am the champion!” he yelled. Then he had to hide behind the shed as Monstermash’s mum came into the garden and began to take in the washing. She frowned. She scowled. She looked all around. Something was missing. She shook her head a few times and went back inside.

Ross grinned. He stuffed the uniform up his jumper and sneaked back indoors. His heart was still thumping like all of the drums in a drum kit, but he felt fantastic. He'd done it! All he had to do now was walk into Top End Primary the next morning.

Aaaaaaaaaaaaaaaaaargh!!!

Ross turned white from top to toe.

What was he saying?

Did he really think he could get away with it? Was he mad? Was he crazy? Would he get killed a hundred times over? Probably.

GULP!

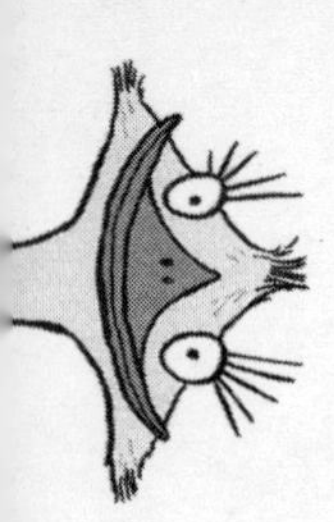

Chapter 15
Ross Gets Even Braver

The next morning was Friday morning. It was the day of the football final. Ross and Katie stood at the corner of the street next to Top End Primary and watched the children going into school.

"They look very big," said Ross.

"You'll be fine," said Katie.

"I look like an idiot in this uniform," Ross pointed out.

It was true. He *did* look like an idiot.

Monstermash was much bigger than Ross. Some people might even say that Monstermash was *too* big. They just wouldn't say it when Monstermash was listening. The trousers were too long and they were much too big round the middle. The sweatshirt was too large and the sleeves dangled a long way past Ross's hands.

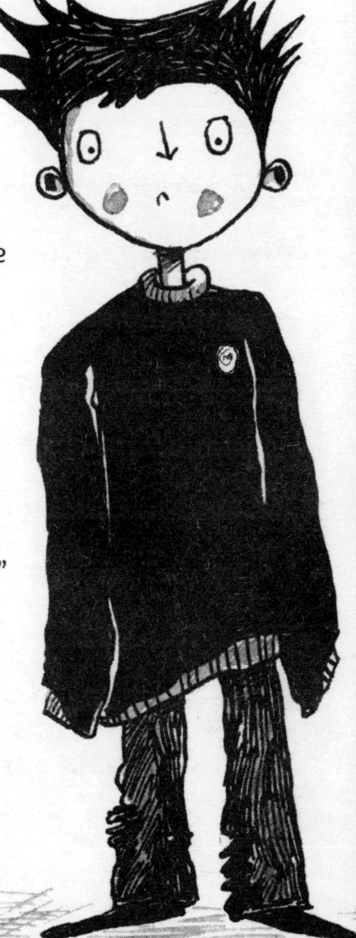

"I'm going to get killed," said Ross.

"No, you're not," Katie told him. "You're going to

go into the school. You're going to rescue Mad Iris. Then you'll be a great hero and you'll be able to marry the princess, just like in a fairy tale."

Ross scowled. "I suppose you're the princess?"

Katie beamed up at him and nodded.

Ross sighed. "I'd better get going," he said.

"Good luck," Katie whispered, blowing him a kiss.

Ross turned very red and shuffled towards the school entrance. At any moment he thought someone was going to grab him and say, "Hey! You're not from our school!"

But he got through the front gate without anyone saying a word. He got through the front door and still nobody stopped him. All of a sudden, Ross began to think that he might just be able to do this amazing thing. He might find Mad Iris. He might rescue her. He might become a hero – a real hero! He might marry the princess.

Noooooo! Nightmare!

He didn't want to marry any princesses!

"Hey! You, boy!"

Ross stopped and swung round. He found himself face to face with Miss Sly, the head teacher. She had a plaster above her eye where she'd been hit by a flying saucer the day before. It made her look a bit like a pirate. She was scary.

"Where are you going? You know the

classrooms are back that way. Whose class are you in?"

Ross was in a panic. He didn't know the name of any of the teachers at Top End. Then, as he was trying to think of what to say, Miss Sly peered closely at him.

"Are those your trousers?" she said. "They look awfully big."

"They're my brother's," Ross said quickly. "I wet mine." Ross gritted his teeth. How could he say such a stupid thing?

"You WET your trousers?"

"I mean I spilled my drink on them," Ross said as fast as he could. "This morning. At breakfast. Milk."

Miss Sly shook her head. "You're a strange boy. Well, don't just stand there pulling faces at me and looking like a prize fool. Get to your class."

Ross turned away and hurried back down the corridor. Phew! A narrow escape.

As he walked, he looked into the rooms on both sides. And there she was! Mad Iris! She was in the ... well, what room could it be? Ross thought it had probably been the library once. Before Mad Iris came.

Mad Iris had grabbed every single book. She'd pecked them and kicked them. She'd thrown them at the windows. She'd thrown them at the walls and ceiling. She'd played football with them. In fact, Mad Iris had done just about everything she could do to them, except read them.

Ross checked that nobody was looking and slipped into the room. Mad Iris was so pleased to see someone she knew. She liked Ross. Ross was fun. She went straight across to him and tried to pull all his hair out.

“Stop it!” Ross hissed. “Don’t worry. I’ve come to rescue you. We’re going to escape.”

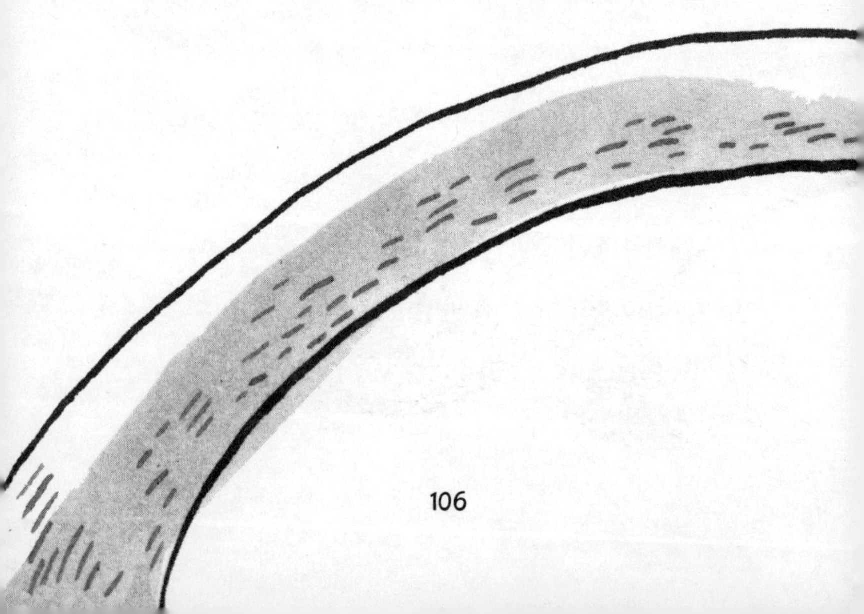

Mad Iris picked up what was left of a book about Vikings and tried to stuff it down the back of Ross's sweatshirt. He swung round and grabbed it from her.

"Stop it!" he said. "Behave yourself."

Ross poked his head round the door. His heart was beating like a drum kit again. He and Mad Iris had to make their escape *now*.

"Follow me," he whispered to the ostrich. "Don't make a sound."

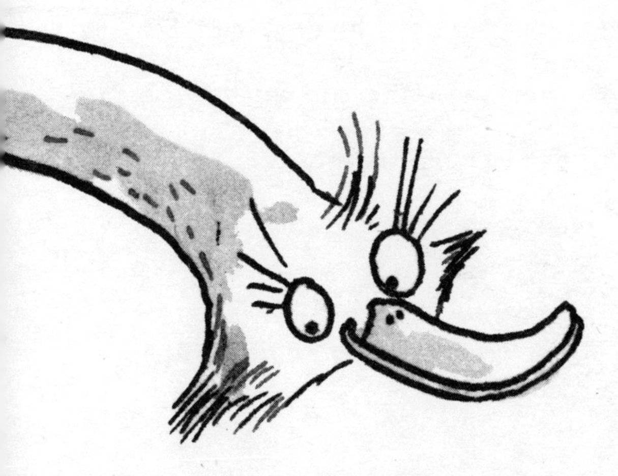

Chapter 16
Ross Gets His Bravery Award

"Come on," said Ross. "Keep very quiet." Iris and Ross stepped into the corridor.

BANG!

What on earth made that noise? It was Mad Iris. She was stuck in the doorway. She had a chair in her beak and she was trying to take it out of the library with her. Ross pushed her quickly back into the room and took the chair away.

"I told you to behave," he said sternly.

"Now, let's try again."

This time they got into the corridor without any trouble. At the end of the corridor was the front entrance and beyond that – freedom. Ross kept his eyes on the front entrance and marched towards it. Just then a classroom door opened and out came a boy. Monstermash!

Monstermash stood right in front of Ross and stared at him. Ross was sure Monstermash would know who he was. Wasn't Ross his next-door neighbour, after all?

"Don't I ...?" Monstermash began.

"No, you don't," Ross said firmly, and he shook his head.

But Monstermash went on staring and staring at him. He stood right in front of Ross, blocking the corridor. Ross couldn't move.

"Aren't you ...?"

"No, I'm not," Ross said, even more firmly.

Now Monstermash peered at Ross's clothes.

“Aren’t those ...?”

“No, they aren’t,” said Ross quickly. “Well, I must get going. Got to take the ostrich to the vet. She’s having her toenails clipped.”

Monstermash looked down at Mad Iris's bony, claw-like feet. She did have very long toenails. He moved to one side. Ross pulled Mad Iris after him and headed on down the corridor. A few moments later he was pushing the front door open and then they were outside. Freedom!

Ross almost ran down the school path, but he kept his cool just long enough. But when Mad Iris saw Katie, the ostrich began to gallop towards her. Katie threw her arms round the ostrich's neck.

"Oh, Iris," she sighed, "it's so good to see you."

Mad Iris was pleased to see Katie too, so she ate Katie's tie. Well, she tried, but it was still attached to Katie's neck, which made things tricky for both of them.

"I did it!" said Ross. "I did it!"

"My hero!" Katie said with a smile, kissing Ross on the cheek.

"Urgh!" went Ross.

After all the dangers he'd been through, he'd been got in the end!

Chapter 17
The Football Final

The football final was held at Pudding Lane.

Mr Grimble had kept Mad Iris hidden until the match started. “She’ll be a surprise,” he said.

Katie and the Pudding Lane team were shocked when they saw how big the Top End players were. They looked enormous and they stood in a row, grinning like tigers at the Pudding Lane team.

“We’re going to get killed,” Buster

muttered. "What kind of flowers would you like on your grave?"

"Poppies," Katie whispered, and the match began.

In fact, Top End were not very good at football. But they were very clever at fouling without being caught. They tried every trick in the book. It wasn't long before Top End had scored three goals and Pudding Lane were 0–3 down.

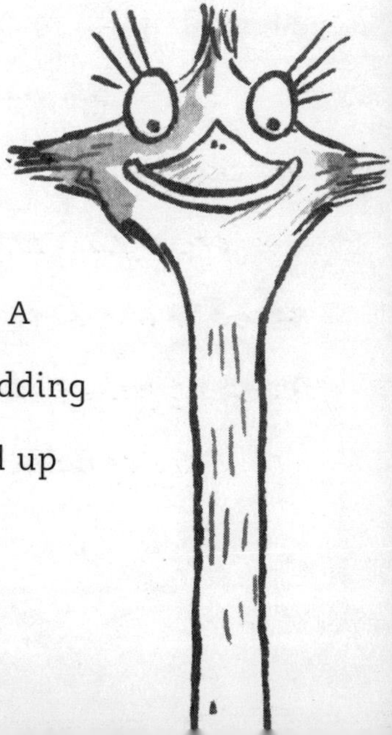

That was the moment that Mr Grimble decided to bring Mad Iris out. He paraded her round the pitch. A great cheer went up from Pudding Lane and the ostrich strutted up and down, eyeing the ball. That football was the most interesting thing that Mad Iris had seen for ages. She did a little dance, pounding the earth with her feet, as if she were getting ready for a penalty kick.

As soon as they saw Mad Iris, the Pudding Lane players got a new burst of life. Moments later, Katie and Buster both scored goals. Now the score was 2–3. Top End were furious. Monstermash fouled Buster. He hacked him so

hard that Buster was put out of the game. He had to be carried off on a stretcher.

Once again Top End were winning and they scored again too. But Katie wasn't giving up and minutes later she scored Pudding Lane's third goal.

Monstermash was furious. "Girls shouldn't play football," he hissed, and he stamped down on Katie's foot. Hard.

"Argh!" Katie crashed to the ground. She hugged her injured foot. It hurt.

"You can't do that!" Ross yelled angrily.

But the ref hadn't seen anything wrong.

"Oh, I am SO sorry." Monstermash smirked. "Did I hurt the little girlie?" he added in a whisper.

Ross helped Katie as she limped to the side. She was out of the game and now Pudding Lane were down to nine players. After that it was a romp for Top End. They scored again and again. Mr Grimble couldn't bear to watch any longer. Neither could the rest of the school and some of them began to drift away from the game. Ross was so angry he didn't know what to do.

But Mad Iris did. She marched onto the pitch and went straight for that wonderful black and white ball. She kicked it. She pushed it with her beak. She raced upfield and ...

BANG!

"Goal!" Ross yelled.

"She can't play!" the Top End players

yelled. "She's an ostrich! Hey, ref – get that ostrich sent off."

But the ref couldn't send Mad Iris off the pitch. There was nothing in the rules to say that ostriches couldn't play football. Ross said that Iris was a substitute for the two injured players. The ref smiled to herself. She was quite happy with that and the game went on.

It wasn't long before the score was 10–10.

There was only one minute of play left. Someone kicked the ball way up into the air. Up and up it went. Everyone rushed towards it, but Mad Iris was ahead of them. She bustled past them all and with one great jump she soared up into the air and ...

BAM!

Mad Iris headed the ball so hard it almost knocked the goalie's head off. The ball shot straight to the back of net.

The referee blew her whistle and that was it – victory for Pudding Lane! 11–10 to them!

The school had never seen such a fantastic victory parade. Everyone was cheering, even the caretaker and the cook.

Miss Sly had to hand over the football cup to Mr Grimble. He wasn't quick enough. Mad Iris grabbed it first and went scampering round and round the school with it. She decided that the cup was hers, and she was right really. After all, she scored the winning goal.

"How's your foot?" Ross asked Katie.

"It's a bit sore," she answered. She was holding an ice pack on it. She gave Ross a winning smile and lifted off the ice pack. "It just needs to be kissed better," she said.

Ross turned white. He would do almost anything for Katie. He had pinched a school uniform from right under Monstermash's nose. He had walked into Top End Primary and rescued Mad Iris. He had faced almost certain death! But there had to be limits.

No way was Ross going to KISS KATIE'S FOOT!

Chapter 18

The Animal Man

But there was something that *everyone* in Pudding Lane School thought was a great idea. In a few days' time a special visitor would be coming to the school. Captain Kapow, the Animal Man, was going to give a talk about animals to the whole school. He was going to bring some REAL animals with him. Captain Kapow was very exciting. He always wrote his name like this –

CAPTAIN KAPOW!!

with two exclamation marks to show children just how exciting he was.

The Year 1s and 2s were 100% certain that Captain Kapow would bring a real giraffe.

The Year 3s and 4s were far more sensible. Anyone could see giraffes were too tall for school. They knew for sure that Captain Kapow would bring a lion.

The Year 5s and 6s told the younger children that there was no way Captain Kapow would bring a lion into school. But they had heard that he had a spitting cobra.

"What's a spitting cobra?" a worried Year 2 asked.

"It's a snake that spits poison at you – SPLLARGH! Like that," Ian Tufnell said. Ian liked scaring people. He did a good job of scaring the Year 2. She burst into tears and said she'd gone off Captain Kapow and his animals and she wanted her teddy.

In fact, none of the children really knew what animals Captain Kapow would bring with him. It was a funny thing, but NOT knowing was even more exciting than if they DID know. In any case, the head teacher, Mr Grimble, had exciting plans of his own. He made an announcement in Assembly.

"I want you to collect as many cardboard boxes as you can," Mr Grimble told the children. "They can be any shape and size – tiny ones, small ones, big ones, *massive* ones. They will all be useful. We will use them to make some life-sized model animals. When Captain Kapow sees them he will be very impressed and think we are the best school in the country."

"In the world!" young Max shouted. He was only just five and liked to call out in Assembly.

"Yes, Max," Mr Grimble agreed. "The best school in the world. Now –"

"In the universe!" Max yelled before Mr Grimble could go on.

"Yes, Max," the head teacher said, and his face turned bright red. "In the universe. Please don't call out in Assembly."

The older children started to snigger. They liked it when Max shouted out things and made Mr Grimble go red.

"Every class will make their own display of animals," Mr Grimble said. "We'll put some of the best ones in the hall where everyone can see them."

"Even aliens!" Max called out.

"Probably not aliens, Max." Mr Grimble sighed, but he was smiling a secret smile to himself. He said a few more things about Captain Kapow and then said the children could go back to their classrooms.

Of course everyone was busy talking about what animals they would like to make models of.

Ross and Katie went back to Mrs Norton's class together. That was because they were good friends – very good friends. Some people said that Katie was Ross's girlfriend. Ross said no she definitely was NOT, but just like Mr Grimble, he said it with a secret smile. (People don't always say what they are really feeling!)

"I think we should make an ostrich," Gloria said.

"We've already got an ostrich, a real one," Kelly Jessup snapped.

As you know, that was quite true. Pudding Lane School *did* have a real ostrich. Mad Iris had escaped from an ostrich farm and now she had lots of fun as the Pudding Lane school mascot.

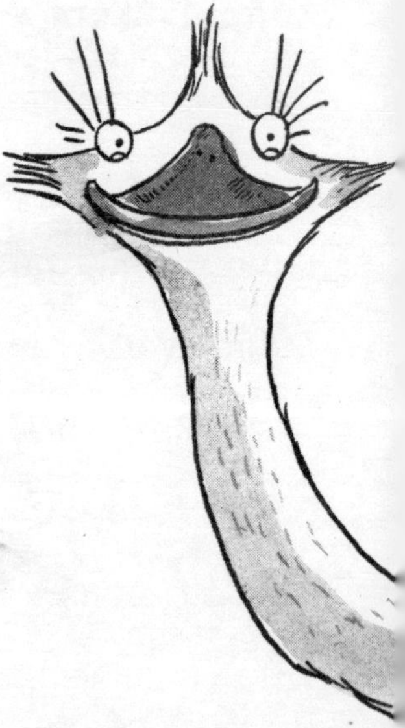

Everyone loved Mad Iris

even when she stole their packed lunches and ate them. Sometimes she ate their gym shoes too, or their ties, or their socks. Once she ate Ross's swimming trunks, and the phone in the school office. Ostriches will eat almost *anything*.

Mrs Norton, the class teacher, had an idea of her own.

"We are going to build the biggest land animal there is!" she said.

The class boggled. The biggest land animal of all? That could only mean one thing. They were going to make an elephant!

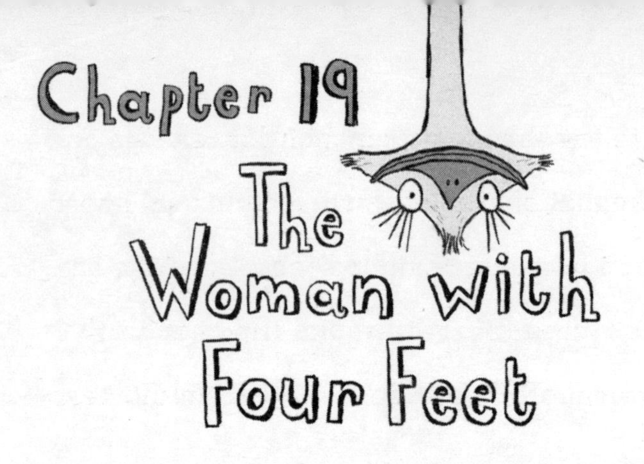

Chapter 19
The Woman with Four Feet

The next morning Mr Grimble stood at his office window. He was staring out at a rather odd sight. First of all there came a procession of children carrying cardboard boxes. Some of the boxes were so big they hid the child carrying them. All Mr Grimble could see was the box and a pair of small feet.

However, there was something even odder behind the children. Mr Grimble watched as a strange creature walked up the path to the school entrance. It looked like a woman, but she was a very peculiar shape. She was bulgy and she had four feet. Yes, Mr Grimble counted them again. It was a bulgy woman with two big feet and two small ones. That definitely made four in total.

A few moments later there was a knock at Mr Grimble's office door. The secretary, Mrs Perch, poked her head round the door. Mrs Perch looked a bit alarmed, but then Mrs Perch often looked a bit alarmed. Even the office computer scared her.

"There's a Mrs Fretting here to see you, Mr Grimble," Mrs Perch announced.

"Fine, fine. Send her in, Mrs Perch," said Mr Grimble.

Mrs Fretting was the woman with four feet. She almost jumped in through the door, as if she was afraid the door might suddenly snap at her. When she was safely in the room, Mrs Fretting opened her extra-large coat. Under the coat was a small child with a pale face and sticky-up hair like a hedgehog.

"This is Charlie," Mrs Fretting said.

"Hello, Charlie, pleased to meet you," said Mr Grimble. Charlie looked at Mr Grimble, then at his mother and then at the head teacher again.

"I want Charlie to come to your school," Mrs Fretting said. "We have just moved to the area. My neighbour said your school was a good one."

"Oh, thank you," Mr Grimble said. "We like to think it is."

"The thing is, Charlie has problems," said Mrs Fretting. "He's allergic. He's got multiple allergies."

Charlie looked at his mum and then at Mr

Grimble. His thin face remained blank.

"Oh dear," Mr Grimble murmured. "Just what is Charlie allergic to?"

"Doors," Charlie's mother said.

"Doors?" repeated Mr Grimble. He was rather surprised, to say the least.

"Yes. They attack him," Mrs Fretting declared.

"Surely you mean he bumps into them, that sort of thing?" Mr Grimble said.

"No. They attack him," Mrs Fretting insisted. "They come flying at him."

Mr Grimble cleared his throat. "I really don't think doors can fly," he said.

Mrs Fretting ignored the head teacher. "I have to keep Charlie under my coat when we go in or out of a door, otherwise he comes up in bruises and bumps. And he's got other allergies too. He's allergic to books and to reading."

"Oh dear," Mr Grimble said with a big sigh. He could see that being allergic to reading could be very awkward in a school – or anywhere else for that matter.

"Yes," said Mrs Fretting, nodding hard. "You put a book in front of Charlie and it sets him off. He just sneezes and sneezes. Sometimes I'm surprised he's still got a nose on his face."

"Oh dear," Mr Grimble repeated. He looked at Charlie again. Charlie's face still had no expression on it at all. He simply looked straight back at Mr Grimble and then at his mother as if he was waiting to see what would happen next.

"And there's one more thing he's allergic to," Mrs Fretting went on. "Ostriches. You don't have any ostriches in the school, do you?"

"Ostriches?" Mr Grimble bit his lip. Oh dear. This was getting difficult. He needed more pupils for the school.

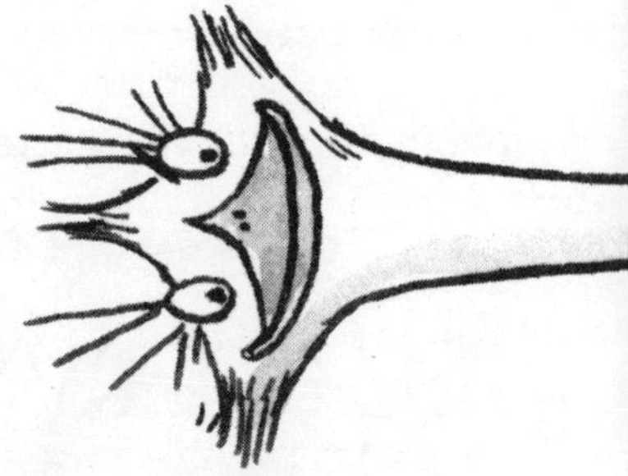

And there was something about Charlie that interested Mr Grimble. He had an odd mother, for a start. Mr Grimble knew that sometimes parents said things about their child that weren't *exactly* true. The child was not always who the parent thought they were.

However, there *was* an ostrich in Pudding Lane School. Mad Iris. What on earth should Mr Grimble say to Mrs Fretting?

Mr Grimble stood up from his chair and beamed a smile at Mrs Fretting and Charlie. "I'm happy to say we do *not* have an ostrich here, Mrs Fretting," he said.

Of course, Mr Grimble was right. He didn't have an ostrich *here*. That was because the ostrich was in the caretaker's shed, over *there*, where she lived, on the other side of the school.

Mr Grimble was also crossing his fingers behind his back.

"We would love to have Charlie at our

school and I am sure he will be very happy here," Mr Grimble declared. His fingers were still crossed behind his back.

"Good," Mrs Fretting said. "Just be careful with them doors. Cover him up when he goes in or out of one. And keep him away from the library and all them nasty books."

"Right," Mr Grimble said with a nod. "We'll do our best."

Charlie looked at his mum and then he looked at the head teacher, just as before. His face was still an empty sheet of paper.

Chapter 20 Bad News

Mr Grimble put Charlie in Mrs Norton's class. Mrs Norton asked Ross and Katie to help look after him until he got used to the school. Ross was surprised when Mrs Norton told him to make sure Charlie was covered with a coat when he went in or out of the door.

"He's allergic to doors," Mrs Norton explained.

Ross was even more surprised when Charlie refused to hide under Ross's coat.

Instead he walked in and out of all the doors in the school without batting an eyelid.

"But you're allergic to doors," Ross said. He wondered if Charlie would come out in spots, or maybe explode.

"No." Charlie shook his head. "My mum thinks I'm allergic to doors, but I'm not. Look."

Charlie walked out of the door, turned round, came back and walked in again. He did that ten times and each time he got through to the other side he made his eyes boggle. He stuck out his arms, waggled his fingers

at Ross and Katie and went "YAAAAA!" in glee.

"When I was three I walked into a door by mistake," Charlie explained. "I got a black eye. Mum thought I was half dead and took me to the hospital even though I was OK really. But ever since then she's been telling people I'm allergic to doors. She also thinks I'm allergic to reading," he went on. "But I love books. And one day my grandad read me a story about an ostrich and I had a sneezing fit. Then Mum started to tell people I'm allergic to ostriches *and* reading, but I'm not. Anyway, I've never even seen a real ostrich."

"We can show you one!" Katie shouted. "Follow me!"

Ross and Charlie trailed after Katie.

"Your mum's weird," Ross told Charlie.

Charlie shrugged. "I think everyone is weird in some way."

"I'm not," Ross said with a laugh.

"Yes you are," Charlie said. "For example, anyone can see you like Katie a lot, but you pretend not to. Why? If I liked Katie I'd want to tell everyone."

Ross frowned. Hmmm. Was Charlie right? He *did* like Katie, but he hadn't realised that people could tell.

"How do you know I like Katie?" he said.

For the first time Charlie's face broke into a

smile. "It's *so* obvious. You look at her as if you want to hold hands with her all the time."

"I don't!" Ross snapped.

"Yes you do," Katie said with a giggle. "Gloria's noticed and Kelly and, well, just about the whole class. Even Mrs Norton knows."

"Mrs Norton!" Ross squeaked.

This was too much! Ross told himself that he'd never look at Katie again, but then of course he looked right at her. He had to. There was no denying it. He *did* like Katie. But Charlie was the first person Ross had met who didn't seem to think it mattered. Ross had a lot to think about.

By this time Katie was dragging both Ross and Charlie across to meet Mad Iris. Katie was desperate to see if Charlie would break out in spots or sneeze all over the place.

But it turned out that Mad Iris liked Charlie almost as much as Ross liked Katie. At least, that is what everyone decided.

She stuck her head down his shirt.

She twiddled his hair with her beak.

And then she undid his laces and tried to eat his shoes.

"She's lovely," Charlie said, and his pale face lit up with a huge grin. He liked all the attention he was getting from this strange bird. He didn't sneeze and he didn't explode either. He did cough a couple of times but that was because Mad Iris had just butted him in the stomach with her head, twice.

"She does that when she likes someone," Katie said with a proud smile as Mad Iris did the same to her and Ross.

"It's her way of saying 'thank you'," Ross explained. "We saved her from the ostrich farm. She ran away and then some men came to catch her and turn her into ostrich steaks, but Katie and I saved her. Then Mr Grimble said the school could keep her."

"Here comes Mr Grimble now," Katie said. "He doesn't look very happy, does he?"

Mr Grimble certainly did not look happy at all. In fact, the children had never seen him looking so troubled.

"Are you all right, Mr Grimble?" Ross asked.

"No. I am not all right, Ross, but thank you for asking," Mr Grimble said. "I have just had some bad news. Very bad news. Inspectors are coming to the school."

"Police inspectors?" Charlie said. "Exciting!"

"No, Charlie. I'd be delighted if they were police inspectors," Mr Grimble said. He had turned as pasty white as spilled milk. "No. These are school inspectors. Three inspectors are coming to inspect our school. And then write a report about us. Oh dear. Oh dear, oh dear. Inspectors. Here, in our school!"

Charlie raised his eyebrows and looked at the others. "I think our head teacher is allergic to school inspectors," he remarked.

Chapter 21 Bamboo Shoots

There were three inspectors. Mr Grimble introduced them to the children in Assembly.

Miss Cactus was in charge. She wore spectacles that looked like gun barrels. She had a black skirt and a black jacket and a

black blouse. Her top half was large and her bottom half was thin and narrow, so she looked like an upside-down triangle.

Miss Cactus liked to ask awkward questions like, "What is a platypus?"

Gloria put up her hand and asked Miss Cactus if it was a cat that had been run over. Miss Cactus said of course it wasn't and was Gloria trying to be funny? Gloria said she didn't think a squashed cat was the least bit funny.

"Then why did you say it?" Miss Cactus snapped.

Gloria turned bright red, hung her head and stared at her knees. Her knees were a lot more comforting to look at than Miss Cactus's face.

Mr Singh had a beard and a turban. When he smiled his big, friendly smile, it showed two gold teeth, one next to the other. He kept a photo of his five children in his jacket pocket.

"These are my children," he told the Assembly with pride. "They are good children. Are *you* good children?"

Ross opened his mouth to say he was good but then he stopped. Just because *he* thought something it didn't mean everyone else thought the same way. After all, sometimes he got into trouble with Mrs Norton. Maybe Mrs Norton didn't think Ross was good. Ross decided it was best to keep quiet, so he did.

Mr Singh smiled. He put the photo back in his jacket pocket and patted it a few times.

The third inspector was called Mr Twine and he was very tall and thin. The sleeves of his jacket were too short, so you could see his bony hands and wrists. Mr Twine didn't say much at all except "Ah!" or "Oh!" or "Hmmmm." He seemed to look at the ceiling a lot. Ross wondered if he was a ceiling inspector.

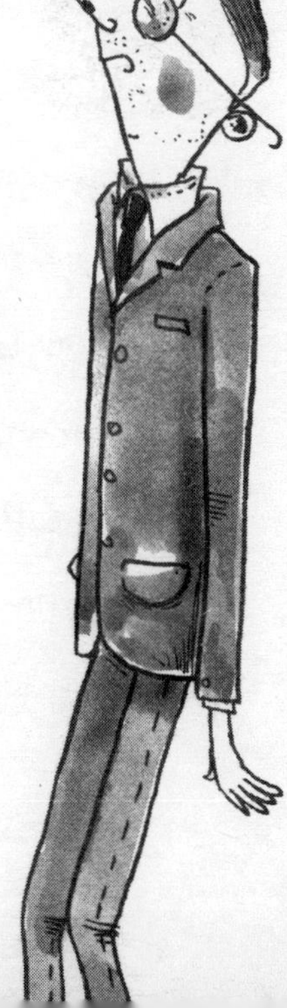

After Assembly, Ross and his friends went back to their classroom. Mrs Norton told them that they were going to make a start on building a cardboard elephant.

"We have lots of boxes," she said. "Well done, everybody. I would like you all to get into your groups."

Mrs Norton sometimes split the class into four groups to do things like P.E. She had given each group a name. They were Cabbages, Peas, Beans and Broccoli. Mrs Norton thought that if the children were named after vegetables they might like eating vegetables more. So far the idea didn't seem to be working, but Mrs Norton carried on all the same.

"Now then, I would like Peas and Beans to build the legs," Mrs Norton said.

Ian Tufnell's hand shot up. He was in the Peas group. "Please, Miss," he said, "the Beans smell."

Everyone burst out laughing, even half the Beans.

"No we don't!" they giggled.

Mrs Norton sighed. "Just get on with it," she ordered. "Broccoli, you can make the body, and Cabbages, you can make the trunk. There."

So that was sorted. Mrs Norton went and sat down. She hoped that the elephant would keep them busy for at least half an hour. But unfortunately, just as they got started, the three inspectors marched in and interrupted them.

"What's going on here?" Miss Cactus asked.

"We're making an elephant," Kelly Jessup told her.

"Why?" Miss Cactus demanded.

"Captain Kapow is coming tomorrow," several children chanted. "He's bringing real live animals!"

"I see," Miss Cactus murmured. She pursed her lips. "Will he bring an elephant with him?"

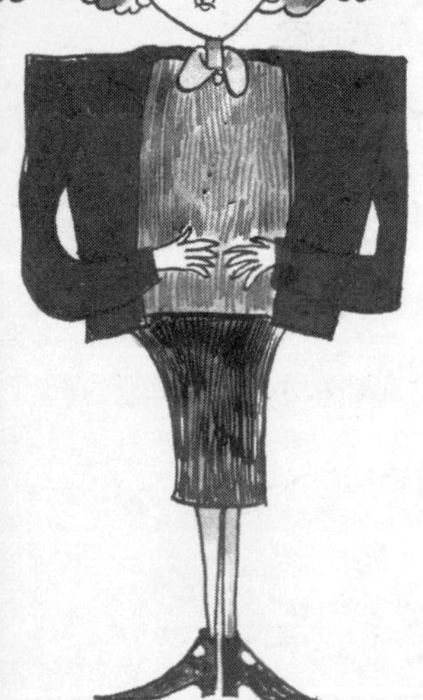

"I think that's rather unlikely," Mrs Norton said with a chuckle.

"Then why make one?" Miss Cactus smiled as if she had just laid a careful trap and it had worked. She had just caught Mrs Norton and a whole class in it.

"Are you going to

measure it? Weigh it? Write about it? Do you know what elephants eat?” Miss Cactus asked. She glared at the whole class.

Ian Tufnell’s hand shot up. “Bamboo shoots!” he shouted.

Mrs Norton groaned.

Miss Cactus groaned.

Mr Singh gave a sad smile.

And Mr Twine said, “Oh,” and looked at the ceiling.

“Giant pandas!” Miss Cactus snapped. “Giant pandas eat bamboo shoots, not elephants!” The inspector turned to Mrs Norton.

“Every lesson must have a purpose,” she said. “It must be written down. We need to know what the aims of this task are. Well?" Miss Cactus eyeballed Mrs Norton.

"I thought the children might enjoy it," Mrs Norton said in a small voice.

"Enjoy?" Miss Cactus squeaked. She looked at the other inspectors with horror. "ENJOY? This is a SCHOOL! You're not supposed to enjoy it! It's not a, a, a chocolate biscuit! It's a school!"

Ross was beginning to feel quite sorry for Mrs Norton. He looked across at Katie and Charlie and pulled a face. If this was what things were going to be like with the inspectors, then he didn't think Mad Iris was going to go down very well at all.

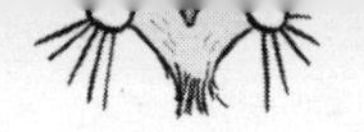

Chapter 22
Where Do You Hide an Ostrich?

At last the inspectors left and went to visit another class in the school. Soon after that a message arrived from Mr Grimble. The message was marked “Top Secret” in big red letters. Mrs Norton read it and looked worried.

“I have a secret message from our head teacher,” she told the class in a whisper. “It says, ‘Don’t let the inspectors see Mad Iris! They will go bananas – especially Miss Cactus, who is allergic to animals of all kinds!’

Including humans," Mrs Norton added, and then she blushed. "You didn't hear me say that," she told the class.

"Yes we did," they answered.

"Oh dear," Mrs Norton said. "Then let's make it a secret between us."

"We like secrets," Katie said, and the class agreed. It was a secret. In fact, it was becoming a very secretive kind of day.

"Yes, but the message has to stay secret too," Ross said. He looked at Mrs Norton. "I think you have to eat it to make sure it stays secret," he told her.

"Really?" Mrs Norton looked at the message. It didn't look in the least bit tasty.

"It's a secret," the class chanted. "You

always have to eat secret messages after you've read them."

"Really?" Mrs Norton said again. "Oh dear."

She ate the message. The class watched her with wide eyes.

"She did it!" Ian Tufnell cried. "She ate the message! Wow!"

Everyone was very impressed. Mrs Norton looked a lot more cheerful as she swallowed the final bit of the message.

"There! It's all gone," she said.

"Mrs Norton's brilliant!" Kelly murmured. Everyone agreed, including Mrs Norton.

But unfortunately just then another problem arrived. It was a very big, ostrich-sized problem. In fact, the problem *was* an ostrich. Mad Iris had escaped from her shed and was on the loose. The whole class saw her dash across the playground.

"We've got to catch her before the inspectors see her!" Ross cried. "Come on!"

And, in the wink of an eye, the whole class had rushed out to the playground and were chasing after Mad Iris.

Of course, Mad Iris thought it was a game and it was a game she liked very much. She raced around pecking at the children and Mrs Norton too. She pecked at their shoelaces. She pecked at their hair. She pecked at Mrs Norton's bottom.

"Ooh!" Mrs Norton squeaked, and she

jumped in the air. "Oh!" she squeaked as Mad Iris did it again. Mad Iris liked making Mrs Norton squeak.

At last Katie and Charlie managed to get hold of the ostrich. They led her over to the classroom and they all went in.

Mad Iris liked the classroom a lot. It was full of lovely, chewy things.

"That's my pencil!" Gloria cried as the pencil disappeared into Mad Iris's beak.

"That's my workbook!" Kelly cried as the workbook went the same way.

"Here! She can eat my workbook too," Ian Tufnell said.

Then Iris saw the cardboard elephant. She lifted her head and eyeballed the elephant.

"I think she wants to eat it," Katie murmured.

Mrs Norton was horrified. She almost

threw herself in front of the elephant.

"No!" she shouted. She wagged a stern finger at Mad Iris. The ostrich took no notice. She just took a step towards Mrs Norton.

Just then Charlie shouted, "The inspectors are crossing the playground. They're heading straight for our classroom!"

Even Mad Iris turned and stared out of the window. For a moment everyone in the class froze. But not Mad Iris. She took the opportunity to have another quick peck at Mrs Norton's bottom.

"Ooh!" went Mrs Norton. "Ooh!"

And if ostriches can smile, then that is what Mad Iris did. In fact, she grinned.

"What are we going to do?" Ross shouted.

Charlie's eyes sparkled. "Hide Mad Iris in the elephant!" he said. "Come on, it's big enough. We can push her inside."

"But the inspectors will see her legs," Kelly Jessup pointed out.

"Everybody stand in front of the elephant," Mrs Norton ordered. "Come on, hurry! That will hide Mad Iris's legs from view."

It was a bit of a struggle to get Mad Iris inside the elephant, but they managed it. Just as the inspectors walked in, the whole class suddenly moved to stand in front of it.

Miss Cactus eyed them, one by one. She seemed to suspect something was up. Her eyes narrowed to slits. “What ARE you doing?” she demanded.

“I am posing the children for a class photo in front of the cardboard elephant we have made,” said Mrs Norton.

“Ah,” muttered Mr Twine.

“I’ve got a photo of my children,” said Mr Singh, and he reached for his family snap.

“But you don’t have a camera, Mrs Norton,” Miss Cactus pointed out.

“I haven’t finished posing the children yet,” Mrs Norton said.

“Hmmmm,” Mr Twine murmured, and he looked at the ceiling.

Miss Cactus sniffed. “Have you got the aims of this work written down yet?” she said.

"We are all working on that," Mrs Norton lied.

"Good. I want to see them by the end of the day," Miss Cactus said. She turned on her heel and all three inspectors headed for the door.

The class heaved a sigh of relief. Mrs Norton heaved a sigh of relief. Everything was going to be fine.

As Miss Cactus reached the door she turned back to the class. And that was when the big cardboard elephant began heading for the door too.

Chapter 23
Mad Iris Takes Charge

Miss Cactus boggled. She wobbled and goggled, and still the elephant came sliding towards her. Finally her nerve broke. She turned tail and fled.

"There's a cardboard elephant chasing me!" she yelled at Mr Twine and Mr Singh.

"Oh," said Mr Twine.

Mr Singh patted his pocket to make sure his children were safe.

Miss Cactus went hurtling past them, still

shouting. She headed straight for Mr Grimble's office and burst through the door like a hand grenade. Mr Grimble almost fell off his chair.

"This school," Miss Cactus panted. "This school – *pant pant* – is a disaster area! *Pant pant*."

Mr Grimble sighed. "Oh dear," he said.

"Yes," Miss Cactus snapped, getting her breath back. "I have never seen such madness. I have just been chased across the playground by an elephant."

"What? I didn't think Captain Kapow was coming until tomorrow," Mr Grimble said.

"It was a cardboard elephant," Miss Cactus insisted.

Mr Grimble was beginning to think that maybe the "madness" was in Miss Cactus's head.

A cardboard elephant that chased school inspectors?

"Surely cardboard elephants can't move?" he asked, quite understandably.

"Go and see for yourself!" Miss Cactus ordered.

So Mr Grimble went out to the playground and Miss Cactus followed. There was the elephant. Mr Grimble approached it carefully. He thought it might try and charge him. But no, the elephant didn't budge.

And so Mr Grimble went right up to it and patted its side. He turned to Miss Cactus and raised his hands in disbelief.

"It's cardboard," he said. "It's made from boxes. It can't move."

"I'm telling you, it chased me," Miss Cactus repeated. "I want you to have it removed from this school at once."

Mr Grimble had just caught sight of

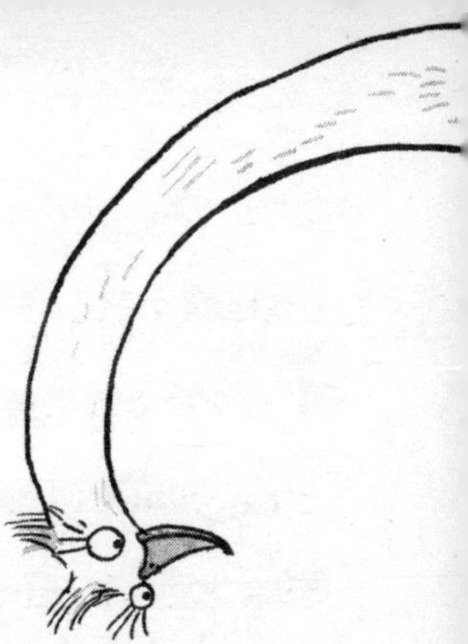

something moving behind Miss Cactus. The head of an ostrich poked out from the corner of a classroom. A child's hand reached out and it was hastily pulled back, but then the head popped out again, followed by the body and the legs. Mad Iris was behind Miss Cactus and she was running straight at her.

"I think you'd better move," Mr Grimble said.

"I am not moving until you sort out this elephant," Miss Cactus shouted. "I am not moving until –"

At that moment Mad Iris screeched to a halt right behind Miss Cactus. Her eyes glinted with delight and with one single peck the ostrich sent Miss Cactus jumping higher than if she'd been on a trampoline.

"Ow!" Miss Cactus yelled. "That was my *bottom*!" As she landed back on her feet she saw Mad Iris.

"An ostrich *and* an elephant! What kind of school is this? I'll see that you get closed down! And then I will report you to the police! Your school is a disgrace. It's a danger to the public!"

Miss Cactus hadn't even finished shouting at Mr Grimble when Mad Iris got fed up with the sound of the inspector's voice. The ostrich started pecking at Miss Cactus's ankles, and then her jacket and her hair. Last of all she grabbed hold of Miss Cactus's nose.

"Let go!" Miss Cactus ordered. So Mad Iris let go and grabbed her left knee instead.

Mr Twine and Mr Singh stood not far away and watched.

"Ah," Mr Twine muttered, shaking his head.

"Goodness gracious me," Mr Singh said. He got out his photo of his children and looked at that. Looking at the photo of his children's smiling faces always helped to calm him down.

"Ow! Ow!" Miss Cactus yelled. "You'll pay for this!" she shouted at Mr Grimble. "The whole school will pay for this. You are in such trouble. I will be writing you the worst school report ever. Get this ostrich off me!"

But Mad Iris wouldn't stop. Finally Miss Cactus made a run for it, heading for the school gate. She reached the gate just as Mrs Fretting came walking in.

"An ostrich!" Mrs Fretting cried. "My poor Charlie's allergic to ostriches! What's going on? Somebody save my Charlie!"

"Somebody save *me*!" Miss Cactus howled.

Mr Grimble watched them all in despair. He put his hands to his head. How many problems could he deal with? What should he do?

Save Charlie?

Save Miss Cactus?

Save the school?

Save himself?

It was all too, *too* much.

Poor Mr Grimble looked up the sky, squeezed his eyes tight shut and yelled.

"AAAAAAAAARRRRRRGGGGGHHHHHH!!!!"

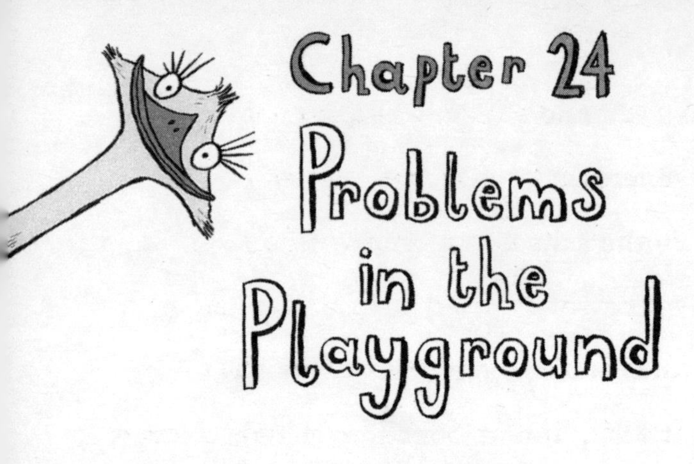

Chapter 24
Problems in the Playground

The next day arrived. It brought thunder, lightning and heavy, *heavy* rain. It also brought the three inspectors and Mrs Fretting.

Mr Grimble saw them coming and tried to hide in his office, but Miss Cactus and Mrs Fretting almost broke the door down.

"We almost died yesterday!" Miss Cactus declared.

"Mad Iris is only an ostrich, she's not a hand grenade or a nuclear bomb," Mr Grimble pointed out. "And she only chased you, Miss Cactus. She didn't chase Mrs Fretting."

"Hmmm," Mr Twine said with a nod.

Mrs Fretting turned purple with anger. "I almost died *too*. I'm allergic to ostriches!"

"I thought it was Charlie who was allergic to ostriches," said Mr Grimble.

"He is, and I caught it off him."

"I don't think you can catch allergies, Mrs Fretting," Mr Grimble said. "They are not infectious." He felt very tired.

"Ah," Mr Twine said with a nod.

"My five children have no allergies, no allergies at all," Mr Singh said with a smile. "The secret is –"

But nobody heard what Mr Singh's secret

was because Mrs Fretting was about to burst a blood vessel with rage. She turned to Miss Cactus.

"Listen to him!" she shouted. "That man thinks I'm *lying*! Me! He should be sacked from his job!"

"I agree," Miss Cactus sniped. "And I'm the one who is going to sack him."

But before Miss Cactus could sack Mr Grimble, she was interrupted by the arrival of Captain Kapow.

Or rather, CAPTAIN KAPOW!!

Captain Kapow was tall, dark and handsome. He had a dashing smile full of bright white teeth. He had a proper suntan that he'd picked up in Africa on safari. He had hair so dark it had to have come out of a bottle.

"Hello, ladies. Hello, head teacher," Captain Kapow said. His voice was like honey with a hint of chilli pepper. He had a twirly moustache and a battered safari hat.

Miss Cactus stared at Captain Kapow and gasped. "Oh!" she gasped. She sounded a bit like Mr Twine, only far less bored.

"Ooh!" Mrs Fretting murmured. She sounded like herself, but in a suddenly good mood. "I think I might faint into his arms. I'm allergic to tall, dark, handsome men. They make me swoon."

Captain Kapow smiled at everyone again. "I've brought the animals," he said. "Should I start unloading them?"

"By all means," Mr Grimble said. "I shall go round the classes and gather the children."

Mr Grimble was very happy. Now he had a good excuse to escape from the clutches of Miss Cactus and Mrs Fretting. They were far too busy admiring Captain Kapow.

Then Mrs Fretting and the inspectors all went and stood under the school porch to watch Captain Kapow unload his animals. It was pouring with rain and the animals didn't like it much. Two monkeys chattered at each other and covered their heads with their small hairy hands. An eagle owl blinked a lot and went "whoo-hoo" in protest. A little crocodile didn't care about the rain at all. A box full of meerkats all stood on their back legs, as if they were hoping someone would pass round some umbrellas.

At last, Captain Kapow lifted out a snake. It was a python, a great big python. Captain Kapow let the snake coil around him.

Miss Cactus gasped. "He's the bravest man I've ever seen!" she whispered to Mrs Fretting.

It was at that point that there was a gigantic flash of lightning followed by a ginormous explosion of thunder right overhead and the rain turned into the Niagara Falls.

The animals hooted and barked and squawked in fear. The monkeys banged against their little cage, and all of a sudden the door sprang open and they were out. They barged straight into the meerkats' box and overturned it. The meerkats shot out and scattered in all directions. Then the monkeys managed to set free the little crocodile.

Captain Kapow charged round trying to catch all the animals. This upset the python and it slid quickly off the Captain's shoulders and made straight for Miss Cactus.

"Save me, Captain Kapow!!" Miss Cactus cried.

"I'm rather busy wrestling a crocodile!" Captain Kapow shouted back.

"Oh!" said Mr Twine.

"Whoo-hoo," said the eagle owl.

"At least my children are safe," said Mr Singh, and he patted his pocket.

The monkeys were now trying to climb up Mrs Fretting.

"I'm being eaten by monkeys," she screamed. "Someone save me. I'm allergic to being eaten by monkeys!"

So there it was.

Miss Cactus was about to be squeezed to death by the python. Mrs Fretting was about to be dinner for the monkeys. And all the while, the storm raged on. Lightning flashed

in all directions. A new thunder roll started even before the last thunder roll had finished. The playground was covered in animals and children and everyone was racing around so much it was impossible to know who was chasing what or what was chasing who.

"Call the Fire Brigade!" Miss Cactus yelled, as the python slithered over her feet

and curled around her legs. "Call the police! Call the ambulance! Call the lifeboats!"

And then, at last the Rescue Service arrived. What was the Rescue Service? Well, actually it was Mad Iris, and riding on Mad Iris's back were Charlie and Ross and Katie. Behind them came the whole of Mrs Norton's class, including Mrs Norton and Mr Grimble too.

Mad Iris kicked at the crocodile until it just gave up and lay down with a sigh. Then Mad Iris rocketed off towards Miss Cactus.

"No! No!" Miss Cactus screamed when she saw Mad Iris the python making for her.

Peck! Peck! Peck! went Mad Iris at the python's head. The snake gave a loud hiss and slithered back to Captain Kapow, who was now sitting in a big puddle and crying. His twirly moustache had gone very droopy indeed and rainwater was trickling off both ends of it. (Mad Iris had already eaten his safari hat.)

Next, Mad Iris had a go at the two monkeys and chased them back into their cage. Ross shut the door on them. Then Mad Iris picked up the meerkats one by one in her beak and popped them back in their box. Katie put the lid on top.

Charlie picked up the rather small and gloomy crocodile and slipped that back in its cage too.

And that was that. Job done.

Chapter 25

The End, and Mrs Norton Does Some Colouring

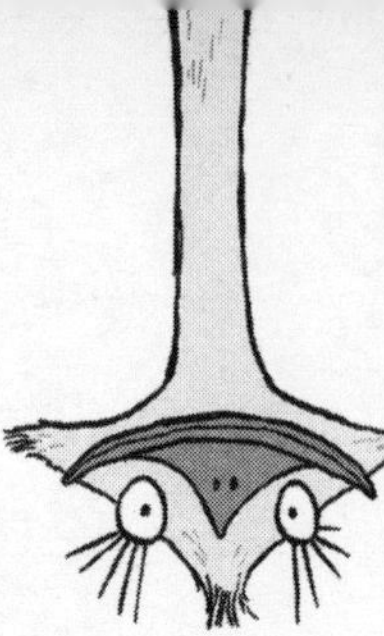

Miss Cactus was in tears.

"I am *so* grateful!" she told Mr Grimble. "That ostrich of yours saved our lives."

"Yes, she did," said Mr Grimble, who was very proud.

Mrs Fretting was staring at Charlie. "You rode an ostrich, Charlie!" she said. "But, but, but – you're allergic to ostriches!"

Charlie looked at his mother. "Mum," he began. "I'm not allergic to anything. You just think I am."

"Oh!" said Mrs Fretting.

"Oh," murmured Mr Twine.

"Well, there's a turn up for the book," said Mrs Fretting. "No allergies at all. I'm very pleased to hear it. So I don't have to hide you under my coat when we see a door?"

"No, Mum," Charlie said with a grin.

"And you're not allergic to reading?"

"I love reading," Charlie declared. "Reading is what I like best."

"Ah," said Mr Twine. "That's nice."

Miss Cactus stared at Mr Twine. "You spoke!" she said. "Two words!"

Mr Twine frowned. “Hmmm,” he hmmm-ed.

Then all the grown-ups went off for a cup of tea and a slice of cake in the staffroom. And the children had to sit in their classrooms and get ever so bored because it was wet play.

At least they weren’t bored for long, thanks to Mad Iris. She decided to go round all the classrooms eating their pencils and trying to tug Ian Tufnell’s hair off his head.

At the end of the day, the children showed the school inspectors their work. They had written stories about Mad Iris and about Captain Kapow's visit. They had painted pictures and written poems and made little books to show their work.

The inspectors were very impressed and they said that Pudding Lane was one of the best schools they had ever been to. Then they went home to write up a very good report, and Mr Grimble breathed a sigh of relief.

And that's the end, almost. But you see, when the children wrote their stories about the storm and the animals escaping, not one of them said anything about how horrible Miss Cactus had been. They were very polite children, you see.

It was Mrs Norton who wrote the true story of the inspectors' visit. You see, Mrs

Norton kept a secret diary and every day she wrote things in it. On this particular day she wrote exactly what she thought of Miss Cactus and how nasty and prickly the inspector had been. Mrs Norton drew pictures too and her favourite picture showed the python squeezing Miss Cactus and Mad Iris pulling her nose at the same time. Mrs Norton even coloured it in.

MAKE YOUR OWN ... MAD IRIS FINGER PUPPET!

Don't worry if your school doesn't have an ostrich mascot – you can make your own mini Mad Iris instead!

YOU WILL NEED

- An adult's help
- Tracing paper
- Thin card
- A pencil
- Felt-tip pens
- Scissors

INSTRUCTIONS

1. Use tracing paper to transfer the puppet shape onto a piece of thin card.

2. Colour in the puppet with your felt-tip pens.

3. Cut around the lines and carefully cut out the circles for your fingers.

How to Draw MAD IRIS!

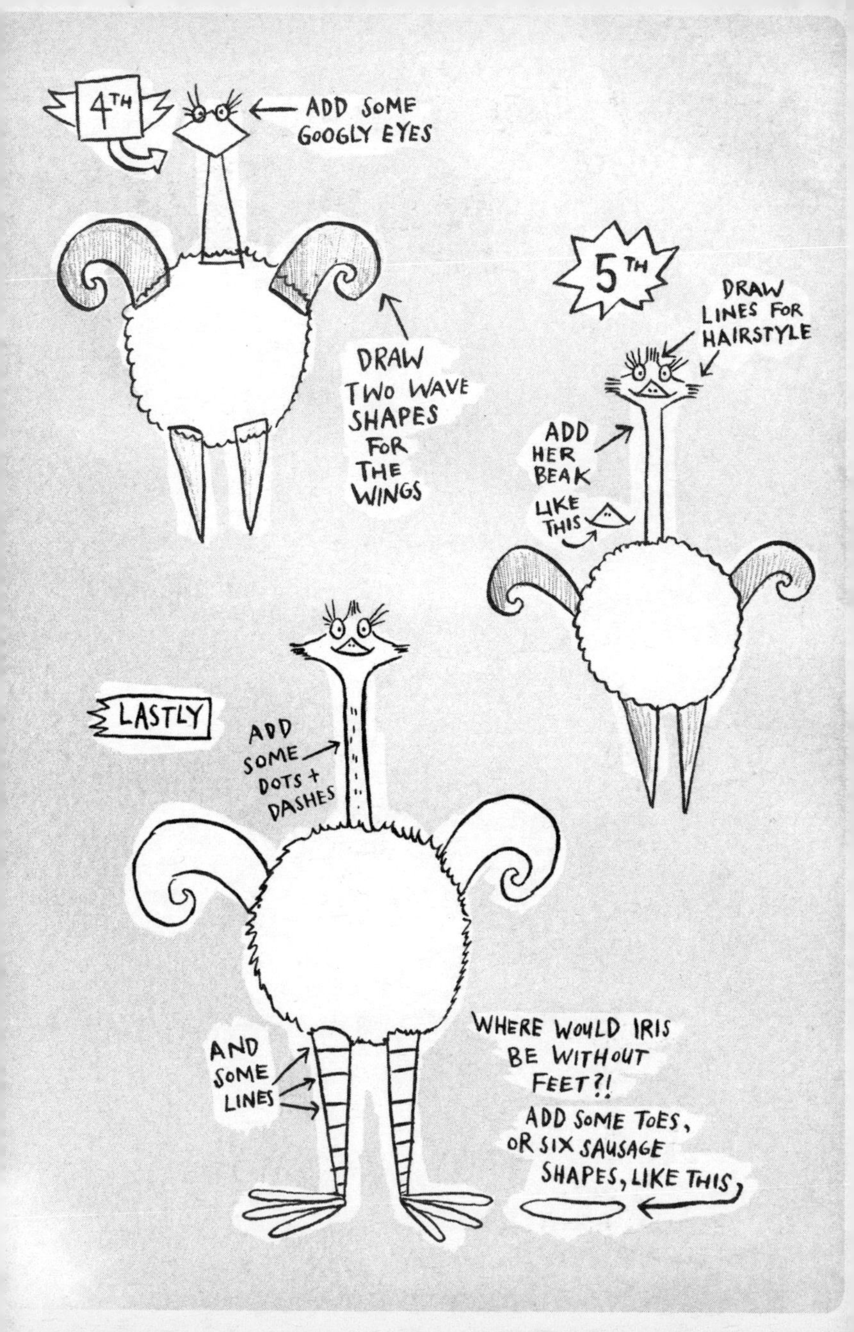
4TH
ADD SOME GOOGLY EYES
DRAW TWO WAVE SHAPES FOR THE WINGS
5TH
DRAW LINES FOR HAIRSTYLE
ADD HER BEAK
LIKE THIS
LASTLY
ADD SOME DOTS + DASHES
AND SOME LINES
WHERE WOULD IRIS BE WITHOUT FEET?!
ADD SOME TOES, OR SIX SAUSAGE SHAPES, LIKE THIS,

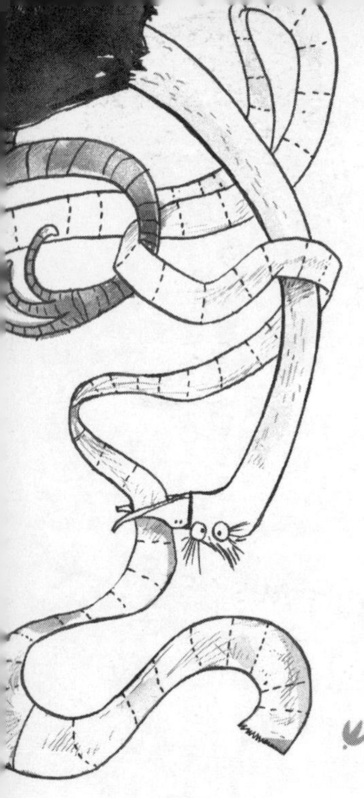

Cheep Laughs!

Make your mates chortle with our brilliant bird-themed gags.

What does the doctor give sick birds?

Tweetment!

When is a good time to buy a bird?

When it's going cheep!

Why did the bird get into trouble at school?

She tweeted on a test!

How do birds build up their muscles?

They do eggs-ercises!

Why are birds' phone bills so big?

They make lots of long-distance caws!

MAKE YOUR OWN ... CAPTAIN KAPOW MOUSTACHE!

Impress your friends with our magnificent cut-out-and-wear Captain Kapow moustache!

YOU WILL NEED

- An adult's help
- Tracing paper
- Thin card
- A pencil
- Scissors
- Felt-tip pens, glue, felt, wool or other decoration

INSTRUCTIONS

1. Use tracing paper to transfer the moustache shape onto a piece of thin card.

2. Colour in the moustache, or decorate it with glue and glitter, felt or wool.

3. Cut around the lines.

4. Stick the back side of the moustache to a bamboo skewer or chopstick with sellotape.

5. Well done! What a magnificently hairy person you are!

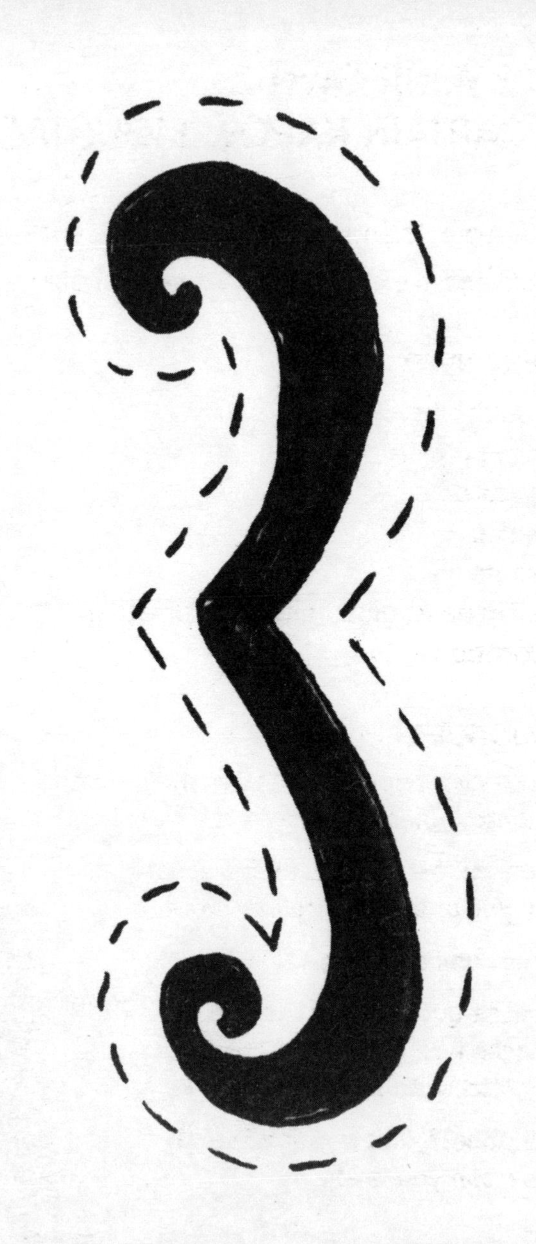

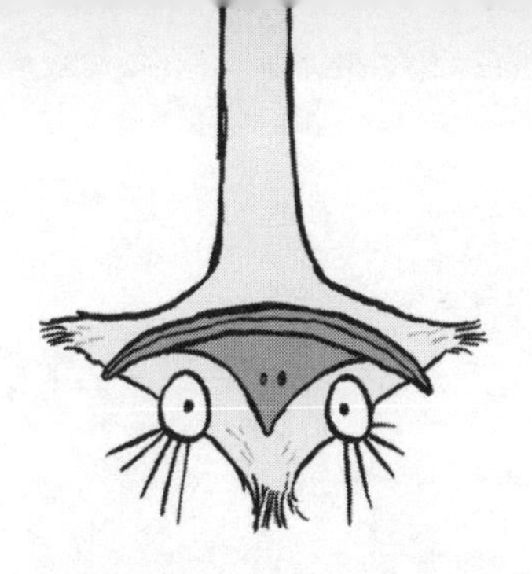

It's OK to EAT books if you're an ostrich like Mad Iris. We're guessing that if you've READ this book, you're not an ostrich ...

And so here are some more fun stories we think you might like to read (NOT eat) ...

Robyn and her Merry Men live deep in
the forest. They wear brown (not green), but they
do like to rob from the rich to give to the poor, foil
dastardly knights, and go on quests ...

This book was written by (Sir) Philip Ardagh,
who takes being funny very seriously indeed.
Writing this book was no laughing matter
(except for the funny parts).

TWANG! DUCK!

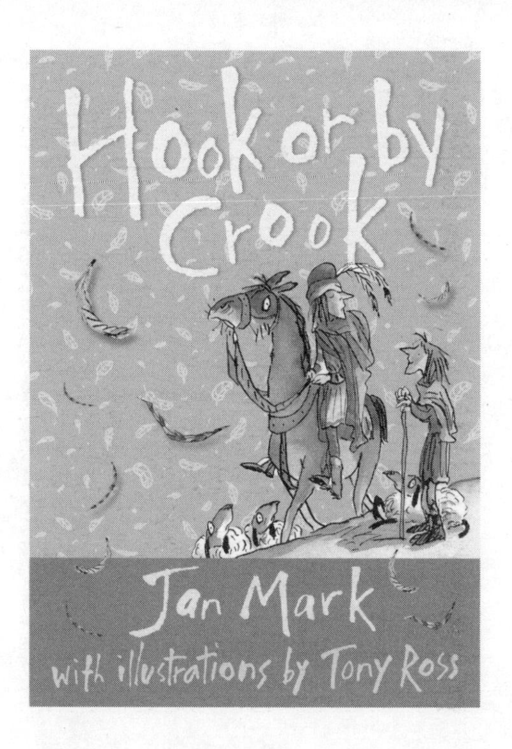

The Abbott of Canterbury is for the chop. Mean King John has set him three puzzles. If the Abbott cannot answer, he'll lose his head.

Robin Hood is about to lose his dinner. He's top outlaw in the forest. But his new career is far from plain sailing!

With foul facts, queasy quizzes and pestilent puzzles, *Hook or by Crook* is Middle Ages mayhem!

Conkers